SHERLOCK HOLMES
MYSTERY MAGAZINE

VOL. 7, NO. 1   Issue #22

SHERLOCK HOLMES
MEETS HOUDINI

MARC
BILGREY

STAFF

Publisher: John Betancourt
Editor: Marvin Kaye
Non-fiction Editor: Carla Coupe
Assistant Editor: Steve Coupe

Sherlock Holmes Mystery Magazine is published by Wildside Press, LLC. Single copies: $10.00 + $3.00 postage. U.S. subscriptions: $59.95 (postage paid) for the next 6 issues in the U.S.A., from: Wildside Press LLC, Subscription Dept. 9710 Traville Gateway Dr., #234; Rockville MD 20850. International subscriptions: see our web site at www.wildsidepress.com. Also available as an ebook through all major ebook etailers, or our web site: wildsidepress.com.

FROM WATSON'S NOTEBOOK

This issue of *Sherlock Holmes Mystery Magazine* offers a single story that I wrote—the tale of the cardboard box—but several other stories are well worth reading, too. I will let my colleague and coeditor Mr Kaye tell you about them.

—John H Watson, M D

✗   ✗   ✗   ✗

Most authors in this issue are what I like to call recidivists since they have appeared here before—Dan Andriacco, Marc Bilgrey. Laird Long and Stan Trybulski. A new story by Eugene D. Goodwin introduces us to Lieutenant Warren T. Sutton, head of the Markheim Colorado police force. In the story of the thief Roebius he is thoroughly baffled by a strange series of bank robberies. Sutton will return with other cases in later issues. We also introduce a "Classic Reprint" department, to showcase rare but exceptional tales by modern writers, kicking off with "The Tahitian Powder Box Mystery," by James Holding.

Finally, thanks to the Rex Stout Estate, the theft of a priceless figurine of a platypus is solved by America's greatest detective Nero Wolfe.

Our 23rd issue will again offer new stories by Dan Andriacco and Laird Long, as well as returning author Steve Liskow. It will also include two Sherlock Holmes adventures and two new Nero Wolfe tales, one by the late Henry Enberg, who used to be on the steering committee of the Stout aficionados group The Wolfe Pack.

See you soon!

Canonically Yours,
Marvin Kaye
✗

ASK MRS HUDSON

by (Mrs) Martha Hudson

Dear Mrs Hudson,

I wonder how you became landlady of 221 Baker Street and whether you were otherwise employed prior to that time?

Curious in Carfax

✗   ✗   ✗

Dear Curious,

The only thing I did before taking over this establishment was to attend school in a London suburb. The Baker Street building was given to my mother to hold for me till I reached maturity. It was a gift from a kindly gentleman named Scrooge. Our co-editor Mr Kaye tells about this in *The Last Christmas of Ebenezer Scrooge*, which was published by the same company that heads this magazine.

Cordial Regards,
(Mrs) Martha Hudson

✗   ✗   ✗   ✗

Dear Mrs Hudson,

As a psychologist I would like to know whether you have ever lost your temper at something Mr Holmes or Dr Watson did?

Henry Vollmer, M D

✗   ✗   ✗

Dear Dr Vollmer,

Dr Watson has never done anything that is not considerate and gentlemanly … I might even say loving. As for Mr Holmes, one must allow for and expect the eccentricities of his genius and in this he never disappoints. I have become mildly distressed on occasion by his behaviour, though he almost always has a cogent reason that he reveals afterward. I was miffed by the noise and damage of his target practice on one of my walls, but he voluntarily added what one may call a remuneration of conscience to the rent for nearly a year.

(Mrs) Martha Hudson

✗   ✗   ✗   ✗

Dear Mrs Hudson,
    Does Mr Holmes ever go on vacation and if so, where?
    Lillian Stackhouse

✗   ✗   ✗

Dear Miss Stackhouse,
    The only time Mr Holmes ever leaves the city and his practice is when Dr Watson insists on it to preserve his friend's health. Unfortunately, no matter where he goes, trouble always seems to catch up with him (them).
    Once they did go fishing in Scotland and brought back a few excellent fish from the river Tay.
    Sincerely,
    (Mrs) Martha Hudson

✗   ✗   ✗   ✗

Dear Mrs Hudson,
    What literature interests your illustrious tenants?
    Gordon Sewald

✗   ✗   ✗

Dear Mr Sewald,
    Mr Holmes devotes most of his time to crime reports in the newspapers as well as whatever news there may be in the criminal world, also justice and law enforcement. He does read philosophy from time to time.
    (Mrs) Martha Hudson

✗   ✗   ✗   ✗

Dear Mrs Hudson,

I have always lived frugally, but recently I won a huge lottery. I did not buy a ticket but found one in the street and picked it up out of the curiosity. To my surprise, it was a winner.

I am both pleased and troubled ethically. I should like to share my windfall with the ticket's original purchaser, but have no idea how to do so. Have you and advice?

Miss Ilene Duguid

✗ ✗ ✗

Dear Miss (aptly-named) Duguid,

I applaud your generous spirit. I asked Mr Holmes and he says you must insert a notice in the newspapers, but he cautions you that frauds will surely surface in great number. If you provide details as to where you found the ticket and what day it was and what time, Mr Holmes will act as your intermediary and find the correct ticket purchaser. He does not expect remuneration for his services.

Admiringly,
Martha Hudson

✗ ✗ ✗ ✗

This issue I have chosen three recipes to share. They are in no way related. I picked them because I'm fond of them all, and so are Mr Holmes and Dr Watson. They are an American dish, broiled turkey; a favourite vegetable, roast fennel, and brandied cherries, of which Dr Watson is fond.

BROILED TURKEY

1 turkey, no more than two months old
5 tablespoons of butter
1 cup of white wine
Salt and fresh-ground pepper

1. Wash, split and dry the turkey.

2. Work in the salt, pepper and two tablespoons of butter.

3. Grease broiler, then put turkey on it and cook till it is brown.

4. Turn over bird and cook till it also browns.

5. Put turkey in a roasting pan and put dabs of 1 tablespoon of butter on it.

6. Boil the wine and pour ¾ cup of it over the bird.

7. Put turkey in oven and bake at 375 degrees till done, occasionally basting it.

8. Pour remaining wine on bird and add rest of the butter, bring to a boil and serve.

✗   ✗   ✗   ✗

ROAST FENNEL

2 fennel bulbs without stalks
2 teaspoons of coconut oil
Lemon juice
Salt and pepper

1. Heat oven to 375 degrees.

2. Put foil in a baking dish.

3. Cut fennel into thin strips.

4. Coat fennel with coconut oil and put into the baking dish.

5. Pour lemon juice on the fennel and add salt and pepper.

6. Heat for 30 minutes.

7. After 15 minutes, turn over the fennel.

✗   ✗   ✗   ✗

CHERRIES WITH BRANDY

2 pounds of dark sour cherries
2 pounds of sweet bing cherries
3 slices of pineapple
2 cinnamon rods
2 tablespoons of cloves
1 cup of sugar
½ cup of Hennessy cognac

1. Remove cherry stems and wash the fruit.

2. Make chunks of the pineapple and add to the cherries.

3. Fill two 1-quart glass bottles with the fruit, leaving space at the top.

4. In each bottle, place a cinnamon rod, 1 tablespoon of cloves and ½ cup of sugar.

5. Pour half of the cognac in each bottle and tightly seal each.

6. After 1 hour, turn each bottle over. Repeat until the sugar cannot be seen.

7. Place the bottles in a cool spot and serve them 4-5 months later.

SCREEN OF THE CRIME

by Kim Newman

SHERLOK KHOLMS

In 2013, writer-director Andrey Kavan made a *Sherlok Kholms* series for Russian television, consisting of six feature-length episodes. It has turned up on youtube with fan-made sub-titles. Its approach to the Conan Doyle source material might once have been considered radical, though now it's almost a default to throw away the deerstalker and the meticulous unflappability to present a stubbled, slovenly bipolar Holmes and a PST-suffering Watson pitted against a chaotic, corrupt world with much contemporary resonance. If you think the BBC's current *Sherlock* is overshadowed by its Watson's hard times in a more recent Afghan war than the one Doyle wrote about, imagine how Russians feel about that blood-soaked patch of the world map. Unlike *Sherlock* and *Elementary*, *Sherlok Kholms* doesn't relocate the characters to a contemporary setting—but it goes further than Guy Ritchie's films in finding Victorian parallels for the way things are today.

In 1979, then-Soviet television produced a fond (and fondly-remembered) *Adventures of Sherlock Holmes and Doctor Watson* with Vasily Livanov and Vitaly Solomin as a genial sleuth and his intrepid sidekick. *Sherlok Kholms* positions itself as radically different from this show, but is structurally rather close to it—with miniseries-like overall arcs to do with the developing relationship of Holmes and Watson and the shadow of Moriarty, and key stories pulled out of canonical order and slotted in to highlight the lead characters. The older show presented its heroes in a nostalgic light—expressing a peculiarly Russian anglophilia—and stressed comradeship and noble endeavour, but the new take is complicated and sometimes uncomfortable. A sub-plot has Watson (Andrey Panin) struggling to become a writer, debating with a publisher about how to make his accounts of thorny real stories more saleable. This suggests that the versions we're familiar with are removed from a truth we are only now being let in on. Throughout, characters say or do things this Watson could never put in print—Watson's marriage proposal to Mrs Hudson (Ingeborna Dapkunaite) is astonishing enough without the throwaway revelation (unthinkable in any British or American Doyle adaptation) that much of the doctor's struggling practice involves performing 'underground abortions'. The approach has some textural precedent in that Doyle has Holmes complain about the way Watson dramatises their cases, but this goes further even than *The Private Life of Sherlock Holmes* or *Mr Holmes* in making its takes on Doyle's characters vastly different from the ones found on the page. There's a sustained riff on the adverse reactions of the people involved when Watson's stories see print: Mrs Hudson resents being represented as 'am old granny' and gives him till the end of the month to get out of 221B ....

The first episode, *Beyker Strit, 221B* (*Baker Street 221B*), opens with exactly the quotation about the Afghan War from *A Study in Scarlet* used in *The Abominable Bride* ('the campaign brought honours and promotion to many but for me it had nothing but misfortune and disaster') as Watson returns to London, 'health irreparably damaged', and is drawn into an alliance with Holmes. In an unusual selection, their first case is 'Black Peter', with Aleksandr Ilin as a suitably imposing, impaled dastard. In suitably dramatic fashion, Watson meets Holmes (Igor Petrenko) over a corpse lying in the street and wind up in separate quarters at 221B. This Watson is balding, moustached and more affected psychologically than physically by the war—and Panin, who narrates and frames each episode scratching away with his pen, is the lead actor here. Petrenko's Holmes looks and acts more like a revolutionary poet than a detective: unshaven, fiddling with rimless glasses, getting drunk rather than taking drugs, treated pretty much as a criminal busybody by the police and flattened in his first 'boxing lesson' with Watson. A very Russian take on male bonding involves hard liquour, pugilism and tears. There's a running joke as Watson assumes several fussy little old ladies in and around Baker Street are his new landlady ... only for the slim, glamorous Dapkunaite to show up at the end (the biggest star in the show, the Lithuanian actress was in *Burnt By the Sun* and has English language credits in *Mission: Impossible*, *Shadow of the Vampire*, *Prime Suspect* and *Wallander*) and strike sparks with the retiring doctor.

Kamen, Nozhnitsy, Bumaga (*Rock, Paper, Scissors*) is a loose adaptation of *The Sign of Four*, which quickly manages to introduce Irene Adler (a lively, lissom Lyanka Gryu), Mycroft (whose face isn't shown—setting up a payoff we have to wait six episodes for) and the malign influence of Moriarty. Here, Watson is involved in the backstory of the Agra treasure as a comrade of the guilty officers—who have returned to London and become a criminal gang, working as cabdrivers to expedite burglaries. Holmes is drawn into the case when Peter Small (Mikhail Evlanov), an old comrade of Watson's, shows up in Baker St badly wounded, taking advantage of the special rates Watson offers for veterans. In the finale, the detective is shut out of a duel at an officers' club between a grim Watson and virulent racist Thad Sholto (Igor Skylar). Your assumptions about the politics of Russian popular entertainment might well be challenged by the way the villain of the piece spouts anti-immigrant/refugee sentiments which sound horribly familiar in the 21st century ... and is roundly condemned for it. The scene has added bite in that several of the extras are visibly and genuinely scarred—are they real veterans of the USSR's Afghan campaign? In a later episode, Watson's publisher tells him to drop the 'chauvinist officer' and the politics and invent a romance to dress up the story. Here, Mary (Elizaveta Alekseeva) is Small's orphan daughter and it's Holmes who sends her an annual pearl (for her board and education) from the otherwise lost treasure; we're to infer that Watson spins this into the love story of *The Sign of Four*, and that the imaginary romance is another thing that irritates Mrs Hudson about Watson's writing.

Only in *Payatsy* (*Clowns*) does the focus start to shift from Watson to Holmes. A key clue in the previous episode is a photograph of the guilty officers taken in Afghanistan, with a shadowy physics professor nearly cropped out. A great deal of time is spent trying to get a full version of the photo as Holmes begins to perceive a single hand behind most of the evil in London. It is personal for the detective in that Irene, who keeps showing up briefly to overturn his composure, is ensnared in the coils of Moriarty. This episode has a magnificently gruesome opening as a wedding photographer is murdered when his flash powder is replaced with TNT, spattering the bride (Natalya Turkina) with gore. The story then revolves around farcical diplomatic business about a fake affair between the American ambassador's naïve wife and a French diplomat which might foment a war between France and America. In a splendid bit of new Holmesianism, the bride is too shocked to describe Moriarty, whom she has seen, and the detective seizes on her profession (fishmonger) to cajole her to think in piscine terms and liken the villain to a pike (long face), crab (eyestalk-like blue spectacles) and an octopus (tentacular arms). This Holmes is anything but immune to emotion—he slaps Watson for calling Irene a whore, and rolls around on the floor in agony when betrayed yet again.

Lyubovnitsy Lord Maulbreya (*The Mistress of Lord Maulbrey*), a case made from whole cloth, features an apparent serial murderer who is eliminating the women who might be mentioned in the will of a wealthy, just-dead aristocrat. It offers a solid, formidable villain in Gilbert Roy (Leonid Timtsunik), who is shockingly violent and ingenious (he favours a poison-dart-firing airgun disguised as a rolled newspaper), and an intriguing *femme fatale* in scheming innocent Ellen (Aleksandra Ursulyak), a gifted artist who presents Holmes with a sketch of the Professor he is looking for. We also learn that Moriarty (Aleksandr Adabashyan), aka Bernard Buckley, smokes distinctive Royal Caribbean cigars. Though Doyle set many stories in London and in rural areas, he oddly neglected to have Holmes work in any of the UK's other cities ... here, the case takes him and Lestrade (Mikhail Boyarskiy) to Bristol, where there's an impressive shoot-out in a hotel and on the street.

It's back to Doyle for the bones of a story in *Obrad Doma Meysgreyvov* (*The Musgrave Ritual*), a detour into the gothic which offers a snowbound Scots castle, a Baskerville-like naïve American Musgrave heir (Aleksandr Golubev), a dour bastard brother (Sergey Yushkevich) who insists even Holmes and Watson wear kilts in freezing weather, a centuries-old family feud, a black-robed ghostly monk (who might evoke Chekhov or Edgar Wallace), the sword of Charles I, Watson delirious with flu and the arrival of the horseless carriage. The most traditional, standalone episode of the series, it might make a useful sampler for folks who just want to give the show a try—getting away from London for a spell means that Holmes and Watson are also away from their ongoing storylines. Suggesting that the makers have a familiarity with previous film and TV takes on the canon, the heir has the character name Reginald Owen, after one of the few actors to have played both Holmes and Watson.

By the time of *Galifaks* (*Halifax*), Watson is a published author—and his work puts him on the outs with an offended Holmes and Mrs Hudson, while the resentful Lestrade is envious of how much the doctor is paid for his stories. With Holmes made famous, Baker Street is thronged with curiosity-seekers and Holmes worries he'll no longer be able to work anonymously. When a corrupt official is glimpsed in a deerstalker and checked cape, smoking a curved pipe, Holmes asks Watson to describe him as looking like that, to get back his ability to work undercover. This begins with a reasonably straight version of 'The Red-Headed League', but the tunnel-to-the-bank business is just Act One of an insanely complex Moriarty plot to heist a printing press from the Royal Mint. The ruthlessness of all parties is stressed—Moriarty poisons the stooges he sends into the bank so they all die during a chase and policemen gun down suspects Wild West fashion. As in *Kamen, Nozhnitsy, Bumaga*, there's a theme about the pride of men in uniform. Lestrade (here, fully named as Fitzpatrick Lestrade) is coldly furious at the members of the police fraternity who have let down the side. Knowing that the constables who have muddy trousers have sold out to Moriarty, he lines his whole force up for inspection and walks past, calmly shooting the traitors. The eponymous Halifax (Andrey Merzlikin), a forger forced to work with the Moriarty gang, specialises in *trompe l'oeuil* tricks—painting a convincing escape tunnel entrance in a cell to alarm a warden—and seems to be making a philosophical point about how trapped and doomed everyone is.

Poslednee delo Kholmsa (*Holmes' Last Case*) opens with Irene in blackface singing 'God Rest You Merry Gentlemen' at a Christmas entertainment at Brasher Castle, which is part of a jewel heist. The script takes a while to get to 'The Final Problem', as it fills in the backstory of Holmes' relationship with Irene in a full-on Paris flashback which involves a meet cute at the base of the unfinished Eiffel Tower, a trip to the Moulin Rouge, absinthe-fuelled sex, impressionist art and a mime. In the present, Watson and Martha Hudson finally stop bickering and he proposes; later, it seems they've become a couple, but not actually got married. The plot goes into full-on bizarre mode with an embassy robbery that exposes a mad science plan involving electrified steel needles which can turn ordinary men into zombie super-soldiers. The face-off in Switzerland features a frozen Reichenbach, much cheating as Moriarty brings a gun and a knife to a (brutal) martial arts fight, Holmes being canny enough to wear spiked shoes while his opponent slides around on the ice and a noise-triggered avalanche which seems to do for both men—prompting Watson to write up a supposed last adventure even though there's one episode to go.

The finale is titled *Sobaka Baskervil* (*Baskerville Hound*), a canny piece of misdirection since the dog only turns up (in a new context) in the final scene, which features a visit to Baker Street by Queen Victoria (Svetlana Kryuchkova). It's three years since Watson wrote of Holmes' death, Professor Challenger is in London lecturing about evolution and young war office clerk Arthur Cadogan West turns up dead in a fish tank in a market (with secret papers on his person) after falling from a train. On the assumption that he knows Holmes' methods, Watson is called in to investigate the crime (derived from 'The Bruce-Partington Plans') in partnership with a nattily-dressed, bearded Mycroft, who turns out to be Sherlock's twin … with the not-dead detective at some point stepping in to impersonate his stuffier sibling to get back in the game. Panin enjoys the chance to play several takes on Sherlock and Mycroft, and the inevitable you're-not-dead shock reunions with the rest of the cast. Moriarty also survived the Reichenbach and—in a development rather like *Sherlock Holmes Game of Shadows*—a key player is cruelly sacrificed to remind us how evil he is. The mcguffin is an ingenious murder contraption wired to the clock of Big Ben (which is either great location work or very good CGI, for a finale reminiscent of the climax of the 1978 version of *The Thirty Nine Steps*). In a Scenes We'd Like to See moment, Holmes launches a furious tirade at the ingenious craftsman who's made the thing for the Professor without caring what he uses it for—remember Doyle's Holmes admiring the workmanship of Colonel Moran's airgun, which has been used in attempts to murder him.

Briefly, in this episode, Holmes puts on a deerstalker and a cape—only to complain that it's uncomfortable. But, by now, he's reconciled to being eclipsed by Watson's version of himself and touched at the title Watson chooses for his book of reminiscences, *My Friend Sherlock Holmes*. So, at the end, after all the reimagining, we come back to what is for this version—as for almost all other versions—the heart of the story, the comradeship of two admirable, difficult men in a world of crime, betrayal, love, honour, diabolic cunning and basic decency.

✗

Kim Newman is a prolific, award-winning English writer and editor, who also acts, is a film critic, and a London broadcaster. Of his many novels and stories, one of the most famous is *Anno Dracula*.

BETTER THAN HOLMES?

by Terry Teachout

This talk was presented to The Wolfe Pack in New York City.

Until now, the only person to whom I've ever had occasion to say the word "werowance" out loud is my wife, so … thank you, Werowance! And thanks to all of you as well. I've been racking my brain in an attempt to come up with a suitable noun of assembly for a gathering of friends of Nero Wolfe—something as good, and as appropriate, as "a murder of crows." It finally came to me just the other day. The Wolfe Pack is an *inquest* of Wolfeans— or, as Inspector Cramer might have put it, a *goddam* inquest of Wolfeans—and I in turn am very greatly honored to have been invited to address this goddam inquest.

Let me begin, then, by laying down a marker: I started reading the works of Rex Stout when I was thirteen years old. I can still remember with perfect clarity how I happened to stumble across Wolfe and Archie. In March of 1969 I read a piece in *Time* called "The American Holmes." It was a profile of Stout, and it led with the highest possible card: "If there is anybody in detective fiction remotely comparable to England's Sherlock Holmes, it is Rex Stout's corpulent genius, Nero Wolfe."

By then I already knew my way around the Sherlock Holmes stories, and so, having subscribed to *Time* in order to widen my cultural horizons, I hopped on my bicycle, pedaled to the public library, and checked out a copy of *Trio for Blunt Instruments*. No sooner did I start reading it than I found myself even more intrigued by the complicated relationship between Wolfe, the orchid-growing, womanhating genius who never left his Manhattan brownstone save under compulsion, and Archie, the wisecracking man of action who did Wolfe's legwork and served as the narrator of their published adventures in private detection.

As soon as I'd finished *Trio for Blunt Instruments*, I went straight back to the library to check out another Wolfe book. Within a few weeks I'd read everything by Rex Stout that they had on the shelves, so I got my mother to take me to the nearest used bookstore, where I bought a slightly tattered paperback copy of *Gambit*. My goal was to collect all of the Nero Wolfe books, no easy task in 1969, at least not for a thirteen-year-old boy living in a small Midwestern town. But I kept at it, and my collection was all but complete by the time I graduated from high school in 1974.

Rex Stout died the following year, a few days after the publication of *A Family Affair*, the last Nero Wolfe novel and the first one that I bought in its original hardcover edition. Now that Stout—and I—had completed the corpus, I naturally started from scratch and read the whole thing again. I've been doing so at regular intervals ever since.

What keeps me, and all of you, coming back? It is, I have no doubt, the fact that the Nero Wolfe novels, like all the best detective stories, are not primarily about their plots. They are conversation pieces, wonderfully witty studies in human character, not so much mystery stories as domestic comedies, the continuing saga of two iron-willed co-dependents engaged in a four-decade-long game of one-upmanship.

Much the same thing can be said, of course, about the Holmes stories. But the great literary critic Edmund Wilson believed that Rex Stout was second best to Conan Doyle—and he didn't mean that as a compliment, either. "Nero Wolfe," Wilson wrote in 1944, was a dim and distant copy of an original. The old stories of Conan Doyle had a wit and a fairy-tale poetry of hansom cabs, gloomy London lodgings and lonely country estates that Rex Stout could hardly duplicate with his backgrounds of modern New York; and the surprises were much more entertaining.

Of course I needn't tell anyone in this room that a great many readers of note have begged to differ with Wilson, and continue to do so. In his lifetime, Rex Stout numbered among his fans such illustrious literary personages as Jacques Barzun, Somerset Maugham, P.G. Wodehouse, and Kingsley Amis. In 1934 Justice Oliver Wendell Holmes, who in his old age had developed what he described as an "ignoble liking" for mysteries, read *Fer-de-Lance*, the first Wolfe novel, and found it to his liking. "This fellow is the best of them all," he scrawled in the margin of his copy.

That said, there can be no possible question that the Wolfe novels were based on the Holmes stories. In preparing this talk, I had occasion to re-read the first half-dozen Wolfe novels back to back, and I was very forcibly struck by the myriad ways in which Stout used Holmes and Watson as points of departure for Wolfe and Archie. I'm not just talking about the obvious borrowings, such as the title of *The League of Frightened Men* or the shared misogyny of Holmes and Wolfe, or the clever but equally obvious ways in which Stout turned Holmes upside down, most famously by making Wolfe fat and sedentary. No, the resemblances go far deeper, in ways both large and small.

As early as the first sentence of *Fer-de-Lance*, Stout is already making teasing reference to Wolfe's earlier, unpublished cases, one of Conan Doyle's own best-remembered tricks. Surely Stout had the Giant Rat of Sumatra in mind when he has Archie "remind" us of "the time the taxi driver ran out on us in the Pine Street case" or "the time [Wolfe] sweated the Diplomacy Club business out of Nyura Pronn." He liked Nyura Pronn so much that he actually mentioned her a second time, in *The Red Box*, although he never did get around to telling us what she was doing at the Diplomacy Club.

Sometimes Stout actually went so far as to crib key plot devices from his great predecessor. The next-to-last "reveal" in *The League of Frightened Men* is borrowed almost literally from "The Man with the Twisted Lip," just as the backstory of *The Rubber Band* is a fairly straightforward variation on the backstory of *A Study in Scarlet*. And speaking of Clara Fox, who can doubt that she is Wolfe's Irene Adler? Archie puts it well when he calls Clara "one of the few women [Wolfe] would have been able to think up a reason for."

Edmund Wilson, then, was right, up to a point: Wolfe and Archie, at least in the Thirties, are closely related to Holmes and Watson. But were they really "dim and distant" copies? Or might Justice Holmes have been right when he called Rex Stout "the best of them all"? Was he thinking specifically of Conan Doyle? That I can't say, but after spending nearly half a century with Wolfe and Archie, I've come to the settled conclusion that the Nero Wolfe novels aren't as good as the Sherlock Holmes stories. No ... they're better. Considered in their totality, they are a vastly more substantial and successful literary achievement, one that I believe to be comparable in quality only to the work of Georges Simenon.

Now I don't want to leave anyone uncertain of my admiration for Sir Arthur Conan Doyle. To have created Sherlock Holmes was a considerable feat of the romantic imagination, and to have paired him with Dr. Watson was a stroke of something not unlike genius. But Conan Doyle, lest we forget, didn't think all that much of his most memorable literary creation. His objection to the Sherlock Holmes stories, and to detective stories in general, was that (in his words) "they only call for the use of a certain portion of one's imaginative faculty, the invention of a plot, without giving any scope for character drawing."

In fact, this objection comes perilously close to inverting the truth about Holmes. The puzzles that he solves are certainly clever enough, but their cleverness exhausts itself on first reading. It is, instead, Holmes the character who fascinates us—and it is his failure to develop other than superficially that is to my mind the principal weakness of the Holmes stories, especially when they're read in bulk.

Anyone who returns to the Sherlock Holmes stories in adulthood after having put them aside for half a lifetime, as I did a few months ago, will likely be startled by this weakness. The Holmes and Watson of *A Study in Scarlet*, it turns out, are already fully developed as personalities, and while we learn a certain number of new things about them in the tales that follow, they do not grow, nor does their relationship alter in any truly significant way. Hence there is no dynamism to the Holmes canon: reading it from beginning to end is not a journey, but a long string of discontinuous events.

Not so the Wolfe novels and stories. It's true that Wolfe and Archie remain the same age, more or less, throughout the series. But they *develop* in a way that Holmes and Watson do not.

I was talking about the first point with my wife the other day, and she put her finger on something that had never before occurred to me. In the early novels, Archie is a very young man—immature, really. It isn't just a matter of his authorial voice not yet having developed fully. He's also immature in his attitudes. Not only is he filial toward Wolfe, but he regards him with more than a touch of youthful hero worship.

As for Wolfe, he's showy, even stagey, forever trotting out the kinds of meant-to-be-quoted aphorisms that the Brits call "made dishes." "I am merely a genius, not a god," he goes out of his way to tell Archie in *Fer-de-Lance*, and we roll our eyes in response, just as we do when he repeatedly asserts that he is an "artist." Real artists don't have to tell us they're artists—we know it already.

Moreover, Wolfe in the Thirties is habitually condescending, at times almost sneeringly so. An all-too-typical example is this exchange from *The Rubber Band*. Wolfe: "Pleasant afternoon, Archie?" Archie: "No, sir. Putrid." Wolfe: "Indeed. A man of action must expect such vexations." You can imagine his tone of voice when he says it, too.

But while these over-obvious traits grate on the sensitive reader, they gradually dry up and disappear as Wolfe and Archie cease over time to be dresser's dummies for made-up affectations and grow into their now-established characters. By the mid-Forties Wolfe has evolved, not dramatically but noticeably—and significantly. His conversation, both on and off the job, has acquired a Johnsonian force and authority that is far removed from the self-conscious posing of the early novels. And when, in *The Silent Speaker*, Archie has occasion to refer to him as a "genius," he does so to Wolfe's face, and he does it not to praise him but to tease him. Wolfe sends Bill Gore to the office of the NIA to "compile certain lists and records," and Archie responds by asking, "Fifty dollars a day for the dregs. Where is there any genius in that?"

Wolfe's response, by the way, is no less revealing: "'Genius?' His frown became a scowl. 'What can genius do with this confounded free-for-all?'" This tells us everything about Nero Wolfe in his maturity. He knows how impressive he is, and so feels no need to assure us of his singularity. Likewise his creator: instead of asserting that Nero Wolfe is an eccentric genius, Stout now *shows* us. The postwar Wolfe burns up a dictionary out of sheer pique. He quizzes his bootblack on classical Greek culture. He goes into hiding, loses a hundred pounds, and grows a beard in order to track down Arnold Zeck—and lets Lily Rowan neck with him to boot!

If anything, the transformation that Archie Goodwin undergoes is even more striking. I have a feeling that Archie, like so many other young men of his generation, was matured by the war in which he served, though the process was already under way by the time he put on his uniform in 1942. Whatever the timing, he's evolved into a noticeably different person when he returns from the war. Yes, he's still a confirmed bachelor who takes love lightly and is quick with a wisecrack. But he's also acquired a touch of gravity, a recognition that the world is a place in which bad things happen to good people, and though he never wears that understanding on his sleeve, it's still visible.

Once again, let's go back to *The Silent Speaker*, the first postwar Wolfe novel, in which Archie meets a classy dame, Phoebe Gunther, and clearly has it in mind to romance her—until the dame in question has her skull caved in by an unknown assailant lurking in the areaway of the brownstone at West 35th Street. And how does Archie respond? He's jolted. *Really* jolted. So much so that when he reflects on how the murderer covered his tracks, he says the following: "Very neat management, I told myself.... Very neat, the dirty deadly bastard." That's serious stuff—not quite Chandleresque, but also not at all the kind of thing Philo Vance would say. It is, in fact, the reaction of a real person, authentic and mature.

And what of Archie's postwar relationship with Nero Wolfe? He's still Wolfe's hired hand, but he's also become an undefinable combination of servant, goad, trusted confidant, and court jester. It's an *uneasy* relationship, intimate but never affectionate. You can still see that Archie loves Wolfe like a father, but it's inconceivable that he'd admit such a thing, or even hint at it. As a result, their intimacy is transformed into a daily contest for dominance—and at least half the fun of the Wolfe books comes from the way in which Stout plays their struggle for laughs, in exactly the way that he might have portrayed a marriage of similarly long standing.

Such relationships lend themselves to close scrutiny, and this is the first and most important way in which Stout surpasses Conan Doyle: we learn more and more about Nero Wolfe and Archie Goodwin as the series progresses, and the more we learn about them, the better we understand them and the more interesting—and human—they become. Compared to Wolfe and Archie, Sherlock Holmes and Dr. Watson are little more than fabulously well-dressed stick figures.

In addition, Stout was also much more sophisticated than Conan Doyle when it came to building into his novels a continuing cast of comparably memorable secondary characters. First come Fred, Orrie, Saul, Fritz, and Theodore, then Inspector Cramer, then Lily Rowan and Lon Cohen—and unlike Lestrade and Moriarty, they are not stick figures but highly distinctive personalities in their own right. Stout could have spun off whole novels about them (and did, of course, with Cramer, though unsuccessfully so). Wouldn't you have gladly read a book about Saul Panzer? But Stout was careful never to tell us *too* much about any of them, not even Saul. He knew who his stars were.

He also understood that Archie is more essential to the artistic success of the novels than Wolfe, and so took care to make him a richer character than Dr. Watson. Archie is also smarter than Watson, and in my opinion a better writer as well. For therein lies the *real* genius of the Wolfe novels—Archie's literary style. It drives the books and is the main source of their enduring interest, and it wouldn't be nearly as effective on a smaller scale.

Which brings us to the last key difference between Rex Stout and Conan Doyle: Stout uses the novel, not the short story, as the basic building unit of his canon. It is, of course, a pleasure to read the Wolfe novellas, but my guess is that most Wolfeans would probably agree that the novels are better, and the reason for this is that they contain more room for character development. In the novellas, Stout is forever cutting to the chase. He has to. In the novels, he has time to digress, to tell us something new about Wolfe or to let Archie sound off on one of his own pet peeves.

I could quote *ad infinitum* to prove my point, but let me settle for one of my all-time favorite digressions. It's from *Before Midnight:*

I would appreciate it if they would call a halt on all their devoted efforts to find a way to abolish war or eliminate disease or run trains with atoms or extend the span of human life to a couple of centuries, and everybody concentrate for a while on how to wake me up in the morning without my resenting it. It may be that a bevy of beautiful maidens in pure silk yellow very sheer gowns, barefooted, singing *Oh, What a Beautiful Morning* and scattering rose petals over me would do the trick, but I'd have to try it.

That's Archie Goodwin to the letter, and in my opinion it beats Dr. Watson all hollow.

And is it art? Of course—not in the same way that Proust and Tolstoy are art, but what of it? Man cannot live by masterpieces alone, nor can any writer, however gifted, hope to produce them every time he sits down at his desk. It is in the nature of things that there must also be well-made pieces of intelligent entertainment to keep our fancies tickled, and that's where Rex Stout came in.

When I wrote about Stout on my blog six years ago, I quoted something that Evelyn Waugh wrote about one of his own characters, a man who wrote detective stories for a living:

"There seemed few ways, of which a writer need not be ashamed, by which he could make a decent living …. to sell something for which the kind of people I liked and respected, would have a use; that was what I sought, and detective stories fulfilled the purpose. They were an art which admitted of classical canons of technique and taste."

That is what Rex Stout did: he supplied his readers with tasteful, intelligent, impeccably artful literary entertainment of a kind that is not merely readable, but *re*-readable—infinitely re-rereadable, in my long and happy experience.

Others have done it as well, but except for Simenon, no one has ever done it so consistently well over so long a span of time— forty-one years, all told. That's an achievement rare enough in any kind of literature and unique in the annals of what H.L. Mencken liked to call "sanguinary literature," one for which I have long been and will always be profoundly grateful. No other writer has given me as much pure, uncomplicated pleasure as Rex Stout. I bless his memory.

✗

Terry Teachout is the drama critic of *The Wall Street Journal* and the author of biographies of Louis Armstrong, George Balanchine, Duke Ellington, and H.L. Mencken. *Satchmo at the Waldorf*, his first play, has been produced off Broadway and throughout America.

"I'M THE OLD MAN"

H.M. AND THE BROTHERS HOLMES

by Dan Andriacco

"I'm the old man," announced H.M., suddenly inflating his chest and assuming an air of aloof majesty which would have done credit to King Edward the Seventh having his portrait painted. "If there's any flumdiddling of the police to be done, I'm the man to do it." A spasm of ghoulish amusement crossed his face.

Thus speaks the unmistakable voice of Sir Henry Merrivale in *My Late Wives* (1946). Vain, profane, atrocious in grammar and outrageous in behavior, H.M.'s penchant for confronting and solving seemingly impossible crimes makes him one of great detectives of the Golden Age of mystery fiction. He is also one of the funniest.

"The Man Who Explained Miracles," as he was called in the title of the only H.M. novelette, sprang from the incredibly fertile mind of John Dickson Carr, writing under the transparent pseudonym of Carter Dickson. Carr is well known to Sherlockians as the author of *The Life of Sir Arthur Conan Doyle* and the co-author, with Adrian Conan Doyle, of half a dozen Sherlock Holmes pastiches in *The Exploits of Sherlock Holmes*.

Although both H.M. and Holmes could be labeled "eccentric" by conventional standards and are both honored by France as members of the Legion of Honor, they would seem to have little else in common. In fact, it would be easy to list the ways in which they are different. Sir Henry is a baronet whose family has held the title for nine generations in a direct line, while Holmes is the descendent of country squires. The baronet is a fighting Socialist in the early days and a member of the Senior Conservatives Club later; Holmes is apolitical. H.M. has a never-seen wife who spends most of her time in the south of France[1], two daughters, "two no good

1   Only in the third to last novel do we learn her name, Clementine, and that she is a blond former chorus girl. "Clemmie's years and years younger than I am."

sons-in-law," and at least one grandson in contrast to the bachelor Holmes. One could go on. A close reading of the Merrivale *oeuvre*, however, leads to the conclusion that Carr's passion for Holmes had a profound impact on the creation of his own detective.

H.M. was born in 1871, making him a younger contemporary of Sherlock Holmes. He sometimes claims that the ancient top hat he sports in the early books (later replaced by a Panama hat, a bowler, or a tweed cap) was a gift to him from Queen Victoria herself, reminding us that he came to adulthood in the Victorian era. Sherlock Holmes, we can be assured from the Sidney Paget illustrations, also wore a top hat on the streets of London. But in *The Plague Court Murders* and *The Unicorn Murders*, the old man has a nickname that evokes the older Holmes brother—some of his underlings call him "Mycroft."

The comparison between H.M. and M.H. goes beyond what Carr frequently calls the baronet's "corporation" (i.e., paunch), the description of his hand in several books as "a big flipper," his fondness for cigars and his Mycroft-like laziness in the early adventures. Like Mycroft, H.M. holds an ambiguous office in the British government. In *The Plague Court Murders* (1934), the first H.M. novel, narrator Ken Blake describes him as the former head of the Counter-Espionage Department who is now "tinkering with the Military Intelligence Department." If Mycroft is the original "M" of the British Secret Service, as many pastiche writers (including me) have posited, then Merrivale is one of his successors.

H.M.'s Mycroft nickname traces back to a letter to Blake from one of the old man's agents in Constantinople. The agent wrote: "I tell you, if our H.M. had a little more dignity and would always remember to put on a necktie and would refrain from humming the words to questionable songs when he lumbers through rooms of lady typists, he wouldn't make a bad Mycroft. He's got the brain, my lad, he's got the *brain* ..." And he employs it solving mostly "impossible" crimes. Whatever H.M.'s title or function at his Whitehall office overlooking the embankment, he is in reality from this first recorded exploit to the last an amateur sleuth and unofficial consultant to Scotland Yard—an unpaid Sherlock Holmes.

Another apparent link to the elder Holmes is Sir Henry's membership in the Diogenes Club, which Mycroft helped to found for the convenience of "the most unsociable and unclubbable men in town." Or is this a different Diogenes Club? Throughout the H.M. series, the old man's membership is almost always mentioned in connection with a certain card game. "Poker players at the Diogenes Club do not get far in attempting to read his face," is how Carr put it in *The Gilded Man*. One wonders how to say "ace in the hole" in Latin—or with no words at all. For according to *The Red Widow Murders*, the inexorable club rule enforced in the downstairs rooms ("except in the Visitors' Room") is: "Herein the brethren shall speak Latin or else keep silent." In Mycroft's club, according to brother Sherlock, the Diogenes had a somewhat different club rule: "No member is permitted to take the least notice of the other one."

At any rate, the Diogenes Club is said to be a good spot for "sittin' and thinkin'," which is how H.M. often describes his method of sleuthing. Whereas Sherlock Holmes personifies logic, H.M. disdains it in *The Unicorn Murders*: "Believe me, I've seen a heap of logical explanations in my time; I know a feller named Humphrey Masters who can give you logical explanations enough to freeze your reason; and the only trouble with them is that they're usually wrong." So what is his method? "Method? Oh, I dunno. I just sit and think." In practice, however, H.M.'s *modus operandi* are closer to those of the Great Detective than this humble description implies.

From early days in his career, for example, Holmes was "a walking calendar of crime," as young Stamford calls him. And the world's first consulting detective put this knowledge of historical crimes to good effect in solving new ones. Here he is doing that in his first case with Watson at his side, *A Study in Scarlet*:

> "Then, of course, this blood belongs to the second individual—presumably the murderer, if murder has been committed. It reminds me of the circumstances attendant on the death of Van Jansen, in Utrecht, in the year '34. Do you remember the case, Gregson?"
> "No, sir."
> "Read it up—you really should. There is nothing new under the sun. It has all been done before."

Again and again over the years that follow, Holmes turns to his commonplace books for details of cases that he remembers filing away. In *The Adventure of the Noble Bachelor*, he calls this "the knowledge of pre-existing cases which services me so well." And then he gives a practical demonstration: "There was a parallel instance in Aberdeen some years back and something on very much the same lines at Munich the year after the Franco-Prussian War."

H.M., too, frequently calls on his vast knowledge of global crime to make observations significant to the solution of the case at hand. Near the end of *Nine—And Death Makes Ten*, for example, he says: "In France, years ago, the very same thing happened by accident: and very nearly cost one woman a whole lot of money because they wouldn't believe she was herself. For years now I've been waitin' for some clever blighter to apply the same dodge to deliberate crime, and lo and behold, somebody has." Just so we know that the old man isn't gulling us, the author cites the source in a footnote—*Clues and Crime: The Science of Criminal Investigation* by H.T.F. Rhodes. (Similarly, *And So to Murder* cites C.J.S. Thompson's *Poison Mysteries Unsolved* to support a precedent to which H.M. alludes.)

Surprisingly, however, H.M. doesn't compare the clue of the missing painting in *The Curse of the Bronze Lamp* to another portrait removed for exactly the same reason in *The Hound of the Baskervilles*. And yet we know that he was familiar with the Canon. In *Night at the Mocking Widow*, the old sinner literally throws a bunch of Russian novels out a window and tells a young girl named Pam to instead "read some fellers named Dumas and Mark Twain and Stevenson and Chesterton and Conan Doyle. They're dead, yes; but they can still whack the britches off of anybody at tellin' a story." About forty pages later, Pam is clutching a copy of *The Adventures of Sherlock Holmes*.

H.M.'s knowledge of the Canon runs deep. He says in *My Late Wives*: "That was where the exquisiteness of this swine's plans struck me in the seat of the pants like Patrick Cairns's harpoon." Cairns is, of course, the killer in *The Adventure of Black Peter*, a Sherlock Holmes story from that memorable year 1895, but that is not an analogy that would occur to a merely casual acquaintance of Mr. Sherlock Holmes.

Interestingly, both H.M. and Holmes evince a curious blind spot when it comes to finding helpful analogies in their own earlier adventures. The illusion that allows Frederick Manning to disappear from a swimming pool in *A Graveyard to Let* is essentially the same one employed by the lovely Lady Helen to vanish in *The Curse of the Bronze Lamp* just three books earlier, yet H.M. apparently never notices it. And if Holmes detected the obvious similarities among *The Red-headed League*, *The Stock-broker's Clerk* and *The Adventure of the Three Garridebs*, he never says so. Nor does he compare *The Adventure of the Six Napoleons* to *The Adventure of the Blue Carbuncle*, *The Adventure of the Second Stain* to *The Naval Treaty* or the first half of *The Valley of Fear* to *The Adventure of the Norwood Builder*.

Another resemblance between the two sleuths is their attitude toward justice. If Mycroft Holmes occasionally *is* the British government, his younger brother often puts himself above the law entirely by letting the criminal go. "Well, well," he quips in *The Adventure of the Three Gables*, "I suppose I shall have to compound a felony as usual." He usually justifies such actions by reference to a higher law. "I suppose that I am commuting a felony," he concedes in *The Adventure of the Blue Carbuncle*, "but it is just possible that I am saving a soul." H.M. allows the criminals to escape in *The Punch and Judy Murders*, *Behind the Crimson Blind* and *The Cavalier's Cup* for a much less elevated reason—he simply happens to like them. In *Behind the Crimson Blind*, he even blows up a ship in the harbor to help the villain (not a murderer) escape. In several other cases he enables a killer to escape in a different way—through suicide.

Beyond the character of H.M. himself, the Merrivale corpus evokes the Canon through both blatant and subtle call-backs in the dialogue.

"You're a regular Sherlock Holmes," observes a character in *The Punch and Judy Murders*. Lady Virginia Brace in *The Cavalier's Cup* challenges Chief Inspector Humphrey Masters with, "Couldn't you deduce that, like Sherlock Holmes, from my first name?" In *The Peacock Feather Murders*, a character asks, "Will you continue with your Holmesian analysis, or do you think it would spoil your effect if I merely confessed?" In none of these instances, be it noted, was the speaker addressing Sir Henry Merrivale.

In *Death in Five Boxes*, the male romantic lead (Carr books always have one, along with a matching female) warns that a certain line of thought would be "theorizing without data." ("It is a capital mistake to theorize in advance of the facts," Sherlock Holmes famously said in *The Adventure of the Second Stain*.) Later, another man in that novel suspects the female romantic lead of being subject to "certain pawky humors." He seems to regard that as a flaw, whereas Holmes clearly meant it as a compliment when he said at the beginning of *The Valley of Fear* that Watson was developing "a certain pawky humour."

Although H.M. himself eschews logic elsewhere, his bookseller friend Ralph Danvers uses decidedly Sherlockian logic in discussing the central problem of *Night at the Mocking Widow* with his old friend of H.M.:

> "If you have stated the circumstances correctly, it is beyond the bounds of human reason and therefore impossible."
> "Uh-huh," H.M. agrees.
> "Then somehow (unwittingly, that is) the circumstances have not been correctly stated!"

Everyone remembers Holmes's often-stated dictum that "when you have eliminated the impossible, whatever remains, *however improbable*, must be the truth." But Holmes also said in *The Adventure of the Priory School*, "It is impossible as I have stated it and therefore I must in some respect have stated it wrong." Surely Danvers must have had this observation in mind.

The Canonical roots of a simple four-word sentence in *My Late Wives* are equally obvious. "I am Roger Bewlay" is almost as dramatic as the powerful "I am Birdy Edwards!" from *The Valley of Fear*. (And is it just a coincidence that one of the victims in *My Late Wives* lived at Crowborough, the East Sussex town where Arthur Conan Doyle lived out his last years?)

When the killer in *The Red Widow Murders* confesses under the false impression that he is going to die and thus insures that he *will* die via hanging, Chief Inspector Masters confides, "And I can't say, between ourselves, that it's very likely to weigh heavily on my conscience." As most of will never forget, Sherlock Holmes says almost exactly the same thing regarding Dr. Roylott's demise at the end of *The Adventure of the Speckled Band*.

Dialogue aside, echoes of Baker Street permeate the adventures of Sir Henry Merrivale in ways big and small:

Bill Cartwright smokes "a curved pipe of the Sherlock Holmes variety" in *And So to Murder*. H.M. also smokes a pipe in some of the early books, although he is seldom seen in the later ones without a vile black cigar. We know from a Paget illustration of *The Greek Interpreter* that Mycroft was also a cigar smoker.

The Cavalier's Cup, in the H.M. novel of that name, is kept in the vaults of Cox & Co. bank in London. This is the same institution where Dr. Watson deposited his battered tin dispatch box with those priceless notes of his unrecorded cases. One wishes that the manuscript of *The Cavalier's Cup* had been left there as well. This is the last and weakest of the book-length H.M. adventures. The supposed comic relief, Signor Ravioli, talks like Chico Marks. "I'm-a-Dr. Watson," he declares, putting on a black felt hat which he seems to think is Watsonian.

Although described as a "whisky-only" or a whisky and punch drinker in other books, the old man and a friend share a bottle of Beaune in *The Red Widow Murders*, evoking Dr. Watson's Beaune-soaked lunch in *The Sign of Four*. And the description of the murder victim's body in *The Punch and Judy Murders* strongly recalls that of Bartholomew Sholto in the same Holmes novel. His bald head is leaned against his shoulder with a grin on his face.

The name of a typist in *My Late Wives*, Mildred Lyons, inevitably recalls Laura Lyons, also a typist, of *Baskervilles* fame. The Sherlockian salute is subtler than the name of the winsome Maureen Holmes in *Behind the Crimson Blind*, but unmistakable nonetheless.

The unconventional, unforgettable Sir Henry Merrivale appeared in 22 novels, one novelette and one short story between 1934 and 1956. Sherlockians would find them well worth seeking out, for there is much that they will find familiar in the wacky world of H.M.

✗

Dan Andriacco, a long-time Sherlockian, is the author of *Baker Street Beat: An Eclectic Collection of Sherlockian Scribblings* and nine Holmes-themed mystery novels and collections. His amateur sleuth, Sebastian McCabe, and brother-in-law Jeff Cody appear most recently in *Bookmarked for Murder*. A frequent contributor to *SHMM*, Dan blogs at www.DanAndriacco.com

ROEBIUS THE ROBBER

by Eugene D. Goodwin

It was my most baffling case, a series of bank robberies and the thief did something so unusual that nobody could believe it, including me.

The robber's name was—is—Roebius. How do I know? He told me so.

My name is Lt. Warren T. Sutton of the Markheim Colorado police force, where I've served for nearly twenty years. Next year I retire.

There are three banks in our town, whose population is about 40,000.

On the morning of April 1st four years ago, a wobbly little fellow (that's how the security guard described him) entered the First Bank and Trust at the corner of Third Street and Brewster Avenue and walked up to said guard.

"Do you see that teller?" he asked the guard. "The last time I was here, he stole five hundred dollars from me."

"He wouldn't do that!"

"Yes, he did. I gave him seven hundred dollars in cash, but when I got the receipt, it only credited two hundred of it. I've decided to talk about this with the bank manager before consulting my attorney. Would you fetch the manager, please?"

"Why don't you ask the teller?"

"I don't want to have anything to do with him!"

"All right. Wait here. But you can see how busy it is. This may take a while."

"That's OK."

So the guard went into the offices at the rear of the room. As soon as he was gone, the complainant—Roebius—approached the teller in question. When his turn came, he placed a leather attaché case on the counter and handed him a note.

READ THIS BEFORE YOU DO ANYTHING OR PEOPLE
WILL DIE!

Place $5,000 and no more or less in this case. You have
one minute to do this. If you exceed the time limit, I will begin
shooting. If you press the security alarm, I will begin shooting.
I will not shoot you, but if anyone dies, it will be all your fault.
You are now being timed, so get going!!!

I still have this note. It was printed by an Epson, not that that's
important.

Well, the teller complied and as he handed the now full attaché
case to the robber, he heard him say, "I'm leaving now. If anyone
in here opens the door to the street in the next three minutes, he
will be shot." Roebius smiled. "Have a nice day."

They respected the time limit and, of course, when they finally
went outside, there was no one there.

✗   ✗   ✗   ✗

I got there along with various police officers and officials, and
we had a lot to do. Questions, interviews, statements written and
signed, but we came up with bupkis, which is usually translated
as "nothing," but my granddad Lew told me it really meant "goat
shit."

When I finally got done, it was time to go home, but my wife
left me last year, so an empty house was not inviting. Instead, I
went to the policeman's home—and office—away from home, the
bar called *Slainté*, which is the Celtic equivalent of "Cheers" and
is pronounced "Slann-jeh," with the second syllable almost whis-
pered. It's a place halfway between the Markheim police station
and my high-rise apartment. The bartender is a fellow in his late
twenties named Benny, but he's wise for someone twice his age,
and he's both my pal and occasionally brother-confessor (being
too callow to be a father-ditto). He looks a lot like Dean Stockwell
when he did that show, *Quantum Leap*, only much younger. Benny
has a ridiculous handlebar mustache and dresses like a sixties hip-
pie. His blue jeans are tattered and patched, which I understand is

the new style. He wears thick glasses; his eyesight is apparently atrocious.

Well, as soon as he saw me, he poured me a generous measure of Johnnie Walker Black on the rocks and asked me what's up. I told him about the bank robbery, and he nodded thoughtfully.

"Bank robbery—the great American pasttime. No one thinks it a real crime. Y'know why?"

"Sure. Everybody wants to pull one off."

"Right," he smiled. "Be right back." Benny busied himself with other customers, but the place was fairly empty, so he got back to me soon. "Any leads?" he asked.

I shook my head. "Nada."

"You'll catch him."

"I'll certainly try." I mulled it over for a moment, then said, "You know, Benny, in most ways this is just another bank job, though I'm not sure if he had a partner waiting in a getaway car. But there's one thing that's very different about this robbery."

He topped off my scotch. "I'm listening."

"He only took five thousand dollars. Here's the note, see?"

Reading it with difficulty, the bartender removed his glasses, squinted, and then his eyes widened. "'No more or less'—well, that's truly weird."

"There's only one reason that I can see for it."

"Shoot."

"It's such a small amount, comparatively, that it's not going to stir up a major ruckus. And this town is big enough to keep me plenty busy, which means if I don't crack this soon, I'm going to have let it slide."

"Warren, I remember you telling me once that it usually takes no more than a week or two to catch a robber because of the trail they leave." He freshened my drink. "This one's on the house."

I thanked him, drained my glass, paid up and then went home, grateful that he'd reminded me of the trail I'd soon pick up and follow.

Only the robber didn't leave one.

⤬   ⤬   ⤬   ⤬

Fast-forward one year. The same date, April 1st. The place: Stevenson Savings and Loan at 435 Hyde Avenue. At about the same time of day, the busiest time, a skinny middle-aged woman entered the bank and walked up to the security guard. (Yes, both banks are small and only feature a single guard at each place.)

"See that teller?" she asked. "The last time that I was here, he made lewd suggestions to me."

"I'm sorry," said the guard, a hefty black gentleman in his early forties, "but why are you telling me?"

"I've decided to complain to the bank manager. Would you get him for me?"

"He's in that office," the guard said, pointing to the other end of the room.

"But I want him to come out so I can watch the teller's face when he sees what's happening."

He sighed. "All right, lady, wait here. I'll see if I can bring him for you." He stepped away. As soon as he was gone, she went to the teller's line and pushed ahead of some irate customers. "Please," she said, "it's a matter of life or death." So, grumbling, they let her go to the head of the line, where she promptly produced an attaché case and a copy of the note that you've already read.

✗   ✗   ✗   ✗

"Benny," I groaned, settling onto a bar stool, "it happened again. This time it was Hyde Savings and Loan."

"The same guy?"

"It must be, though he was disguised as a woman."

"How much did he get?"

"The same. Five thousand."

Benny put the bottle of Johnnie Black on the counter and a bucket of ice. "Take as much as you want for twenty bucks. You obviously need it."

✗   ✗   ✗   ✗

This time, though, the robber got cocky enough to send me an e-mail (probably so that I couldn't work on his handwriting). It said, "Dear Lieutenant, after causing you so much trouble for the last year, I think it is only polite to introduce myself. My name is Roebius, pronounced Ree-bee-us. I'm sorry for the inconvenience I've been, but if you have patience for a while longer, I think you will be pleasantly surprised."

Well, maybe he wanted to be caught. After all, knowing his last name (I doubted that it could be his first), I now had something to work on. I checked on the name Roebius and found two of them in city limits: Jean Roebius MacFarlane and Benedict Roebius. I checked on her first.

Jean lived on a tree-lined street in the suburbs. Her name sounded familiar, and that's because she was married to one of my old deputies, now retired, Hank (Henry) MacFarlane, who was now the watchman at the Markheim Falls shopping mall. On a hunch, I went out to the mall and lucked out because Hank was having lunch with his wife. She was a slim older woman, not so much beautiful as handsome, and she wore a checked dress and warm smile.

"My maiden name was an error when my great-great-grandfather came to America. His name," she explained, "was Richard Moebius, a direct descendant of the man whose name is best known for that peculiarity, the Moebius strip. Now my great-great-granddad, I'm told, always wrote his name as R. Moebius, and that somehow got mangled by a doubtlessly overworked customs official into Richard Roebius, and that's been the family name ever since."

I thanked her for the story and asked whether she knew the other Roebius in the city, Benedict.

"Why, sure!" she told me. "He's my uncle. He lives—let me think—oh, yes, somewhere on Freeman Avenue near the pasta factory. I haven't seen him for a while, but he's a dear. Doesn't get around, though."

"Why not?"

"He was wounded in Viet Nam … or somewhere in the Orient. Needs a wheelchair and—this is terrible!—the same explosion that ruined his legs took away his eyesight."

So it was highly unlikely that he was my thief. Still, I looked him up and went out to visit him. He was an amiable old duffer with a grey mustache and a sweet smile. He did, indeed, sit in a wheelchair, one of the modern variety that could take him almost anywhere, if it were not for his inability to see. I asked him if he had any relatives living in town and he said there were two.

"There's my niece Jean."

"I've met her. She sends you her love."

"What a dear girl! And her husband is a good man." He fumbled in his bathrobe.

"May I help you?"

"No, that's all right. I just wanted a breath mint. I'm afraid I didn't brush my teeth this morning."

"That's all right, I'm not close enough to tell. Now you said you have a second relative in town?"

He nodded. "My son. But I don't know where he is. From time to time, he drops in and brings me things—food, beer, clothing. But he never lets me know where he lives, and I don't have his phone number. It's rather frustrating."

"What's his name?"

"Carter. I named him after President Carter, who I once met. A fine man."

I wasn't that much closer to a solution, but because this Carter Roebius didn't even let his dad know where he lived, I decided provisionally to tag him as my bank robber. His pa described him for me: medium height, brown hair and eyes, and the friendliest of smiles. When I asked his father what his son did for a living, he said he didn't know what his current job might be, but he used to be a ... *bank guard.*

Aha!

But that's the extent of what I managed to milk from the name. Months passed and I turned to my attention to other constabulary duties. And then it was a year later.

✗   ✗   ✗   ✗

There was only one more bank left in Markheim Colorado, so I assigned all of my available men to surround the building, known as the H & H Bank, officially the Hawkins Hamish Bank & Trust, on April 1st.

Nothing happened.

After waiting it out for most of the day, I returned to the police station just before six p.m. and found a message waiting for me that said, "Happy Birthday to me!" which suggested Roebius's birthdate. His father confirmed it, so now I was certain his son was the man I was looking for.

I was about to go home, when the telephone rang. It was Benny the bartender. "Warren, could you come over here? Somebody left a package for you."

"Who? Can you describe him?"

"Short guy. Nothing unusual about him."

"Wait for me. I'll be right over." I treated myself to the luxury of a taxi and was at the *Slainté* in less than fifteen minutes. Benny greeted me. "It's in the back room."

I went in there alone and found a tattered brown attaché case. Next to it were two envelopes. The first bore the printed inscription: READ ME IMMEDIATELY, THEN OPEN THE CASE. The second envelope said OPEN ME LAST.

Well, I really wanted to see what was in the case, but first I tore open the envelope and read this:

> Dear Lieutenant, the only reason I did all this was because I was bored. I wanted to see if I could bring it off and not be caught. Now that I've done it, I have no more use for the contents of the case. With admiration, C. B. Roebius.

I snapped the attaché's latches and found inside it $10,000 in cash. When I ripped open the final envelope, I was not surprised to find it contained two items: a pair of thick eyeglasses and a handlebar mustache.

C. B. Roebius … Carter Benedict Roebius.

I never caught him.

Not that I tried very hard.

✗

Gene Goodwin is a fan of Colorado, since that's where he learned to love TexMex food.

A CLOWN AT MIDNIGHT

by Marc Bilgrey

Jack Miller woke up in the dark, breathing heavily and sweating. He'd had the nightmare again. He looked at the luminous digital clock on his night table. It was four thirty in the morning. He knew that getting to sleep again would be difficult. It always was. When he could get back to sleep at all.

Hours later, Jack walked through the icy February wind and into Benning's Art Store, yawning and rubbing his eyes. His boss, Mr. Stevens, was behind the counter helping a customer when he noticed Jack. Stevens asked an employee to take over for him, and directed Jack into the back office. Stevens sat behind his desk, as he motioned for Jack to sit down on a chair in front of him.

Stevens asked Jack if he knew what time it was. Jack shrugged and said that he thought it was about ten thirty. Stevens told him it was eleven and that the store opened at ten. Stevens frowned and said that had this been an isolated incident, he might have been able to overlook it. But Jack had been late four times in the last month and as a result he had no choice but to let him go.

Jack considered responding, but knew it was pointless. If he told the truth it would just make him sound crazy. Stevens told Jack that he would send him his last pay-check then dismissed him. Jack left the office, walked through the store and outside to Fourteenth Street.

As he went past fast food restaurants, luggage stores, and discount electronic shops, it occurred to him that he should feel awful but instead he only felt numb. If anything he was surprised that he'd lasted as long in the job as he had. Two months was a record for him. Usually, he only made it for a few weeks before he was fired. He wondered what he would do now. In this economy even finding a minimum wage job wasn't that easy. He yawned, then went down a set of stairs into the subway, and took the train uptown. When he got to his apartment he pulled off his clothes, got into bed and took a nap.

✗ ✗ ✗ ✗

That night, Jack met his friend Mike Phillips at a local Chinese restaurant. Mike worked in the circulation department of a neighborhood newspaper. After they ordered dinner, Mike took a gulp of his diet Coke and said, "You'll get another job."

"It's not that," said Jack. "It's the underlying problem."

"You're not going to start with that dream again, are you?"

"It's not a dream, it's a nightmare. How about a little sympathy?"

"Jack, I've been giving you sympathy for over twenty years."

"I know, and I appreciate it. I'm upset."

"Here," said Mike, handing Jack a Post It note.

"What's this?"

"It's the name and number of a hypnotist. Someone at my office went to see her, she helped him quit smoking. She does sleep problems, too."

Jack looked at the little yellow piece of paper and frowned. Could anyone really help him? Over the years he'd tried self-help books, exercise, meditation, talk therapy, and positive affirmations. He'd had high hopes for each one but none of them had worked. He couldn't help being skeptical. After such a long time he was resigned to never getting any better.

Despite his doubts, Jack called Dr. Jennifer Anders the next day. It turned out that she had a cancellation and was able to see him that afternoon. At four o'clock, he walked into her West Side office and sat down on her couch. Dr. Anders was a pretty blonde in her thirties, dressed in a white blouse and black skirt. She smiled warmly and sat down on a chair opposite Jack.

"How can I help you?" she asked.

"I have a lot of trouble sleeping," said Jack, " and because of that, I can't hold down a job, or even have a relationship."

"That doesn't sound good."

Jack took a breath. "It's all because of the nightmare."

"The nightmare?"

"Yeah, uh, you promise you won't laugh?"

"Of course I won't laugh."

"I'm chased by a clown."

"A clown."

"Yes. Big red nose, white face, floppy shoes, blue hair."

"How long have you had this nightmare?"

"My whole life."

"What happens in the nightmare?"

"It's dark. He chases after me. Then he grabs me and puts his hands around my throat and begins to choke me. As I start to black out, I wake up."

"It sounds horrible."

"This nightmare has destroyed my life. It's turned my days into a tired existence. It's made my nights unbearable. I'm always exhausted and depressed."

"Do you have any idea where the nightmare comes from?"

"No. I've never had a problem with a clown. Although I am terrified of them."

"Well, it's no wonder, considering."

"I've been to a psychologist."

"What did the psychologist say?"

"He gave me a lot of double talk about my anxieties. I saw the guy for six months. I got nowhere with him. That was five years ago. I still have the nightmare, sometimes four or five times a week. In a good week I'll only have it two or three times."

Dr. Anders blinked and said, "In the short term I think I can help you get some sleep, but to have a real lasting effect we need to get at the underlying cause."

"If you could really do that it would be great," said Jack, yawning. "But I've had a long history of being disappointed."

"The psychologist probably asked you about trauma."

"Yes, only I couldn't remember any. My parents treated me well, loved me. I was an okay student, no problems with bullies."

"Military service?"

"No."

"Victim of a crime?"

"No."

"Sexual abuse?"

"No."

"Violence?"

"No. My parents never hit me. "

"How about other kids?"

"No."

"Ever been in an accident?"

"No."

"Problems with love?"

"Like I said, it's hard to maintain a relationship if you can't get much sleep."

She nodded, then said, "You mentioned that the psychologist talked about your anxieties. That suggests that he might have been implying that your mind was making up this nightmare based upon any phobias you might have."

"Do you think that's what's happening?"

"Maybe, but rather than your phobias I'd like to explore your unconscious mind."

"My unconscious?"

"Yes. It's possible for the mind to take an actual incident that really happened, that was so traumatic, so disturbing, that it couldn't deal with it on a conscious level, and then bury it in the unconscious. In a sense, it's a kind of self-induced amnesia that the brain creates as a form of protection."

"A repressed memory."

"Exactly. But it's in there and it wants to get out; and the only time it's free to do that is in the dream state."

"The psychologist never suggested that this nightmare might have really happened to me."

"I'm not a psychologist. I look at things from a different perspective."

Dr. Anders had Jack lie down on the couch and close his eyes. She told him to relax and picture himself lying on a tropical beach on a secluded island. She suggested he feel the warm sunlight on his face, the texture of the sand, the smell of the salty air. Within minutes Jack felt himself slipping into a tranquil, surreal state.

✗　　✗　　✗　　✗

Dr. Anders didn't get to the bottom of the mystery during that first session, but after Jack left her office he felt relaxed, and that night slept unusually well. During the next few days, in between searching job sites on his computer, Jack thought about the hypnotist and wondered if she could really help him, or would she just turn out to be another dead end like everything else he'd tried. He decided that he'd give her a chance, just as he'd given all the others who'd tried to help a chance, but he wasn't expecting much.

A week later Jack went back to Dr. Anders for his next session. She had him lie down on her couch again and close his eyes. She asked him to start counting backwards very slowly from one hundred. Then she had him visualize being twenty years old, and then nineteen, and eighteen. Within a few minutes, he saw himself at fifteen, and then at ten. There were birthday parties, school classrooms; he was on a swing at a playground, running through a sprinkler on a lawn, and then was back at the house that his parents rented on Long Island during summers when he was a child.

He was seven years old, wearing a t-shirt and sneakers, getting on a bus that took him from his parents' house to a day camp by the ocean. When he arrived at the camp, he got off the bus and saw his counselors and other kids. Everyone was excited because that day they were going on a field trip to the boardwalk.

The other kids got on the bus and Jack did, too. After a short ride, the bus pulled up at the beach and everyone got off and went to the boardwalk. Jack and the kids went on a children's roller coaster, which he thought was very cool. Then Jack and the kids walked into an arcade, where he heard the sounds of pinball machines and smelled fresh popcorn. Jack played skeeball and won enough tickets to get a small plastic dinosaur. Then the group went outside and the counselors stopped in front of a fun house maze. The grown-ups said that when the kids went into the maze that they should stay together so nobody would get lost. The adults would meet them when they got out. Jack went into the maze with the other kids. It was dark and creepy. He saw his reflection in the mirrors, making him look tall and short. And then suddenly Jack realized he was alone. He'd somehow gotten separated from the other kids. He was scared, crying and couldn't find his way out. He yelled for help but no one heard him. Everywhere he turned there was another mirror.

And then someone grabbed him. Jack couldn't see who it was, only the person's white gloves. Jack tried to pull away, but the hands held him tightly; and then they were around his neck, squeezing his throat. He couldn't breathe. He managed to look up at the face of his attacker. It was a clown. He had a white face, big red lips, and blue hair. Jack heard a woman calling his name. The clown looked frightened and let Jack go. Jack fell to the ground and everything went black.

The next thing Jack knew he was outside in the sunlight, lying on the boardwalk. Counselors were standing over him. Jack felt groggy. He sat up slowly and was given a cup of water. He heard the counselors talking.

"He's okay," said one.

"Luckily we found him on the floor of the maze," said the other.

"Must've fainted," said a third.

"Good thing we noticed he was missing."

"Let's not tell anyone about this."

"We could get fired."

Dr. Anders brought Jack out of the trance, and he opened his eyes.

"How are you?" she asked.

Jack sat up slowly, catching his breath. "I'm okay," he said.

"Are you sure you're all right?" asked Dr. Anders.

"Yes," he said. "I saw him, the clown. I was in a fun house and he found me alone. He would have killed me if he hadn't gotten scared and ran."

"What are you feeling?"

"Scared and relieved. I can't believe that I've been walking around with this experience most of my life and didn't know it."

"There's your nightmare."

"It really happened."

"Yes, but you're safe now. He can't hurt you."

"Who was he?"

"I don't know who he was, but I know what he was."

"What?"

"A repressed memory."

✗   ✗   ✗   ✗

That night Jack slept peacefully. The next morning, he woke up refreshed. It was the first time he could ever remember feeling that way. It was like being reborn. He took a shower, got dressed, shaved, ate some toast, a couple of fried eggs, and went out for a walk. Then he thought about the clown. If Dr. Anders's theory was right, now that he was aware of what had happened, he'd be able to let go of it. Was it really possible, after all these years, that he'd finally be able to sleep well every night?

As he walked down Broadway in the bright sunlight, Jack wondered why he wasn't feeling happier. By all rights he should be ecstatic, celebrating his new found freedom. And yet, despite the number of years that had passed, he couldn't stop thinking about how close he'd come to death. It was only by chance that he'd been saved. A few more seconds of being choked and he would have died.

On 66th Street, feeling dazed, Jack went into the subway and took the train to 42nd. He got out and walked to Fifth Avenue, where he entered the library and went upstairs to the microfilm section. He asked a librarian if she had a newspaper from Beachton, Long Island. She looked it up, then told him that they didn't carry it. She asked him if he might be interested in *Newsday*, which covered all of Long Island. Jack filled out a call slip for July and August of the year when he was seven. He presented it to the librarian, who gave him a few small boxes. He took them to a machine, threaded up the film, and sat down.

He spooled through advertisements featuring men and women wearing old clothes and photos of ancient-looking cars. There were editorials about local politics and pictures of forgotten movie stars, and then he found a small article with the headline "Child Found Dead in Beachton." The piece recounted an incident that had happened on the boardwalk. A six year old boy had been separated from his parents and later found dead under the boardwalk. Official cause of death was still pending, pursuant to the coroner's report, but police at the scene believed it to be asphyxiation from being choked.

Jack printed out the story then went through more reels of microfilm. He found another story about a seven year old boy who was found dead near the arcade, also from asphyxiation, cause pending. Jack printed the second story, then returned the microfilm to the librarian and left the building.

He felt queasy as he walked west toward the subway. The idea of looking in the library had come to him on a whim. He'd wanted to see if his experience had been an isolated incident or whether there were others who hadn't been as lucky as he was. But now, having discovered this information, he was deeply disturbed. Two other boys, both near the maze. Both dead. When Jack got to the subway steps he was so shaky he had to grip the handrail extra hard, for fear that he would fall.

✗   ✗   ✗   ✗

That evening, he sat in his apartment trying to figure out what to do. After a few minutes he picked up his cell phone and texted his friend Mike, telling him what he'd found out both at the hypnotist and from the library. He didn't expect to hear from Mike for a while. Mike was always working and usually took a few days to get back to him.

Jack thought about making something to eat, but instead went out to take a walk. He wandered the streets for a few hours, thinking about his own experience and those of the two boys he'd never met. He imagined them walking through the maze and the white-gloved hands around their necks. Jack decided he needed to find out more for his own sake and for the boys who were never given the chance to grow up.

✗   ✗   ✗   ✗

The next morning, Jack left his apartment, went to Penn Station and bought a round trip ticket to Beachton. A half hour later he stepped into a train and found a window seat. As the train pulled out of the station, Jack wondered what he was going to do when he got there. He wasn't sure. All he knew was that he felt compelled to go.

For the next hour and a half he watched houses, factories, billboards, and trees go by. Then warehouses, gas stations, quaint little towns, and ugly small villages. When the train pulled into the Beachton station Jack got out. The train departed quickly, leaving him alone on the quiet platform. He walked across the tracks and saw an old man sitting on a bench, reading a newspaper. Jack asked him where the beach was. The man looked up at Jack as if he were the dumbest human he'd ever seen, then pointed and went back to his newspaper.

Jack walked along empty streets, past houses with peeling paint and overgrown lawns. In a few minutes the boardwalk came into view and beyond it the ocean. A cool winter breeze was blowing as he climbed the wooden steps that led to the deserted boardwalk. The beach was barren except for a few seagulls.

All the shops and restaurants were closed for the winter. As he walked he thought about that day, a lifetime ago. It was a strange feeling, being back after so many years. What if the arcade no longer existed? And even if it did, it would be closed this time of year. How could he ever hope to find the clown? Then he thought about the other two boys. He owed it to them to keep going.

Jack found a boarded up building where the arcade had once stood. There was a 'for rent' sign on it which gave the name and address of a local real estate company.

✗   ✗   ✗   ✗

The Azore real estate company was located in a house just off Main Street.

Jack walked inside and saw an overweight woman with dyed blond hair, wearing a white blouse, sitting in front of a computer. She turned to face him.

"You in the market for a house?" she asked.

"No, I'm interested in a store on the boardwalk."

"Which one?"

"It used to be an arcade."

"You want to rent?"

"Actually, I'd like to find the previous tenant."

"Excuse me?"

Jack realized that he couldn't tell the woman the truth about why he wanted to locate whoever ran the arcade and maze. He didn't want to sound like someone who might be dangerous. He had to come up with a plausible-sounding explanation.

"Uh," he said, "my family used to spend our summers here when I was a kid, and I have fond memories of the arcade and maze. I'm writing a book about the boardwalk and I was hoping that I could interview whoever ran the arcade."

"You're a little late for that. He died two years ago."

"Oh."

"But maybe his daughter could help you. I'm not really supposed to give out personal information."

"A book about the area could help bring tourists here."

"Now that wouldn't be a bad thing," she said, smiling, as she wrote something down on a pad, then tore off the page and handed it to Jack.

⚒   ⚒   ⚒   ⚒

Marie Denning, who looked only a few years older than Jack, was dressed in a pink blouse and standing outside her beauty shop, smoking a cigarette and checking the messages on her cell phone, when Jack walked up to her and explained who he was and why he was there.

"A book, huh?" she said, blowing some smoke from the side of her mouth. "You write any other books?"

"No, but I have so many good memories of those summers …."

"A poor man's Coney Island is what it was. My pop was always trying to make the big score. He was kind of a dreamer."

"I liked the maze."

"Yeah, I used to work in the maze when I was a teenager."

"Oh?"

"Sure. All kinds of crazy stuff happened in there."

"Like what?"

"One time a guy proposed to his girlfriend in the maze. Go figure. Another time, some pickpocket tried to hide in there. The cops had to go in and look for him. Wouldn't you know it, the cops got lost. But eventually they caught him." She laughed.

"Do you remember a clown with blue hair being in the maze?"

"You mean my Uncle Morty?"

"White face, white costume, big floppy shoes, blue hair?"

"Yeah, that's him. My father's no-good brother. What about him?"

"Did he work there?"

"Sometimes, when he couldn't get a circus job. He would scare people in the maze. My pop thought it would give customers an extra thrill. The truth is Morty was a miserable drunk. I guess I shouldn't say that, but when I was a kid he used to give me the creeps. He's in his late eighties now. He called me a few months ago to hit me up for money. Can you believe it? When I was a kid he wouldn't even buy me an ice cream and now he's begging me for a hand out. Not that it's a surprise. He was always mooching off my pop. I guess my dad felt sorry for him. Besides the drinking,

Uncle Morty also had a little problem with the horses, if you know what I'm sayin'. Some people never change." She looked at Jack and said, "But you don't want to hear about him."

"Actually, I'd like to interview him. I think getting a clown's perspective would be interesting."

"Why waste your time? Besides he's all the way down in Florida. He's been retired for years."

"Do you know where I can contact him?"

✗   ✗   ✗   ✗

When Jack got back to the city, he went to his apartment and texted his friend Mike. He told him what he'd found, and that he was going to go away for a few days. He promised to call him when he got back.

That night Jack got eight hours of peaceful, uninterrupted sleep. When he woke up he felt rested, energetic, and determined to pursue his goal. After dressing, he filled a luggage bag with a change of clothes, his electric shaver, and a toothbrush, then left his apartment and walked two blocks to a bank. He went inside and withdrew nine hundred dollars from his account, his entire life savings. Then he took the train to La Guardia airport.

Jack was in a plane, thirty two thousand feet in the air, when he decided to kill the clown. The idea popped into his head while he was looking out the window at sunlight shining through some clouds. It was as if it had been divinely inspired. Someone had to avenge the dead. It was beyond what the law could do, but that didn't mean that there would be no justice. Jack would be the judge, jury, and executioner. The victims would not be forgotten. He alone could balance the scales. He wasn't sure how he was going to do it. He just knew that he would find the predator and decide on a method when the time came.

Jack had seen true crime shows, had read articles; he knew that these kinds of people never stopped. He was certain that there'd been other victims. Being in the circus was the ideal job. The clown was always in different cities. Who knew how many murders he'd committed?

The plane landed at the Tampa-St. Pete airport. Jack rented a car and began driving north. It was ninety degrees outside. He turned on the car's air conditioner. The cool breeze felt good against his skin.

He drove past fast food places, cheap motels, gas stations, used car lots, farm stands selling oranges, and souvenir huts peddling t-shirts, plastic alligators, and snow globes filled with miniature imitation palm trees. It was if he'd entered another world. Yet, there was something about the shabby kitschyness of the place that made him feel oddly serene. He was David in the land of the Philistines.

Two hours later, Jack saw a sign that read "Tibbsville next exit." He turned off and drove down a two lane road. He went by houses that had brightly painted trailers parked on their front lawns. One had iron bars on it and a live lion inside. He drove past a man walking on a wire that had been strung between two trees.

A couple of minutes later, Jack saw a white-haired woman who looked like she was in her seventies, wearing a gold sequined dress and a silver cowboy hat. He stopped and asked her for directions. She told Jack where to find the street he was looking for, then asked him if he was going to the fund raiser. When he told her that he was a tourist and didn't know about it, she explained that once a year the town put on a circus for a week to raise funds for itself; everyone in town participated, and he was in luck, as it was going on right now. Jack thanked her and drove off.

Ten minutes later, Jack found the street he was looking for and then located the house. He parked across the street. It was a ranch style house. The paint was chipping and the grass on the front lawn was overgrown. Under some weeds was a rusted bicycle. Jack wondered how he'd recognize the man. He'd seen him in dreams for years, and in the regression in the hypnotist's office, but never without his make-up.

Jack's thoughts were interrupted by the front door of the house opening.

A half a dozen clowns, in full make up and costume, walked out. There was a tall one, a short one, a fat one, a skinny one, a sad one, and one with blue hair. They walked to an old sedan, got in, and pulled out of the driveway. Jack waited for a few seconds, then followed.

The sedan went past quiet residential neighborhoods and then through the main street. Jack kept pace with it, but hung far enough back so as not to be seen. Five minutes later the clown's car came to a wide open field outside of town. There was a huge circus tent, with a banner across it that read "Tibbsville Circus." There were at least two hundred cars parked on the grass near the tent. The sedan pulled up, the clowns got out and walked into the tent.

Jack pulled up a few cars away from the sedan, parked, and got out. He asked a man selling tickets when the clowns went on. The man told him that there were clowns throughout the show. Jack bought a ticket and went inside. During the next two hours, he watched acrobats, lion tamers, jugglers, elephants, human cannon balls, horses, and clowns. The crowd applauded and cheered constantly. Jack left before the final act and went back to his car. A short time later, the clowns walked out of the tent, got into the sedan and drove away. Jack followed them. A few minutes later they pulled up to a roadside bar. Jack watched the clowns get out of their car and go into the bar. He waited a few minutes, then left his car and headed to the bar.

The place was packed with circus people, including a bearded lady, a ringmaster, acrobats, and lots of clowns. There were framed circus posters on the walls, and country music blaring from an old jukebox. Jack sat at the bar where he could watch the blue-haired clown. The clown sat at a table with his friends, drinking, laughing, and grabbing every woman who went by.

Three hours later, the clowns paid their bill and stood up. Jack went to his car, got inside and waited. He watched the clowns stumble out of the bar and over to their car. They got inside, swerved onto the road, and drove off. Jack tailed behind. A few minutes later, the sedan stopped in front of the house where they'd come from. The clowns got out, said their goodbyes, and walked off in different directions. The blue-haired clown went into his house and shut the door.

Jack sat in his car and waited. A few minutes went by, and then he saw the lights in the house go off. He let another twenty minutes pass, then quietly got out of his car and went around to the side of the house. He took a pencil flashlight from his pocket and used it to guide himself through the darkness. He checked a couple of windows, but found that they were closed and locked, however, in the back of the house he saw a sliding door and noticed that it was slightly ajar.

He slid the door open and stepped into the living room. There was ugly brown wall-to-wall carpeting on the floor, an old couch, and a few worn chairs. On the walls were some paintings of crying clowns. Jack crept through the hallway and found the bedroom. The door was open and he heard snoring coming from inside. Jack saw the man passed out on the bed, still in his costume and makeup. His blue wig was on a nearby night table. He was bald. Jack felt nauseous as he stared at the man and inhaled the stench of cheap wine that permeated the air. At that moment he wanted to hack him to bits with an ax, but this feeling immediately gave way to a sense of calm and purpose. This was not about emotion, he assured himself: he was there as an instrument of justice.

Jack went over to the bed, noticed a pillow on the floor and picked it up. He held it for a minute, then slowly moved it to the man's face and pushed it down hard. He felt the man struggle, but he continued to hold the pillow firmly. The man flailed like a drowning insect then went limp. Jack gave it a few more seconds before pulling the pillow away. The man now stared at him, glassy-eyed and motionless. Jack looked him over for another minute, making sure there was no further movement. Satisfied, he left the bedroom, walked through the living room, opened the sliding glass door and went back outside. He felt a sense of accomplishment. His mission was complete.

Jack felt his hands quivering as walked around the house and his legs were weak and unsteady. A few wars ago it would have been called battle shakes. He bumped into a garbage can, sending it crashing to the ground. Bottles and beer cans skittered onto the cement. A man walking a dog saw him and yelled, "Hey rube!"

Jack tried to cross the street to get back to his car, but the man was already on him, grabbing him.

"What're you doing around here?" he asked.

"I was just taking a walk," said Jack.

"Is that so?" replied the man.

The noise had attracted other men from nearby houses who came out to see what was the matter.

"I caught this guy on Morty's property," said the man who held onto Jack.

"I'll go see if Morty is okay," said another.

The second man went around the back, then quickly came out of the house through the front door. "Morty's dead," he said.

Jack broke free of the man's grip and ran.

"After him!" yelled one of the men.

"He's getting away!" yelled another.

Jack bolted through the clown's backyard, jumped over some hedges and sprinted down an incline into a wooded area. He heard the men yelling in the distance behind him. He went deeper into the forest, past gnarled, twisted trees. Somewhere in the darkness an owl hooted. Dead leaves crunched under his feet. He came to a clearing and in the misty moonlight saw a cemetery. The gravestones were weathered, cracked, and the grass around them was tall and yellowed.

He heard the men getting closer. Jack saw a mausoleum the size of a one-car garage in the distance. He ran to it, sweating and panting, and with all his strength pushed against the structure's heavy stone door. It slowly creaked open and he went inside the dark chamber. Then using his full weight, he managed to push the door shut behind him.

The place was pitch black and smelled dry and musty. He crouched down against the cold stone wall and listened. He heard the men's muffled voices outside.

"He must be around here someplace," said one.

"Spread out," said another.

"We'll get him," said a third.

After a few minutes Jack heard them come back again.

"Well, he's not here," said one of the men.

"Let's go that way."

"He can't have gotten far."

Then their voices faded. Jack waited a couple of minutes, and switched on his tiny flashlight. He saw a stone wall with square compartments from floor to ceiling. Each one had a name etched into it. He went over and read them:

Arthur Barnes, 1925-2000, a great clown
Ferd Barnes, 1900-1960, a clown for the ages
Brian Barnes, 1897-1952, a clown's clown

Jack walked to the door of the mausoleum and shined his light on it. There were no handles or knobs. He ran his fingers along each side, hoping to find a latch or something that would allow him to pull or push it open, but found nothing. In fact it now looked and felt as solid and unmoving as the other three walls that surrounded him. It was as if there had never been a door there at all.

Jack sat down on the marble floor and took his cell phone out of his jacket pocket. He'd gotten a text. It was from his friend Mike. It read:

"I've looked into the stories of the children who died of asphyxiation in Beachton, when you were seven. The articles you read were only preliminary findings, written during the summer. According to follow up articles that were published a few months later, the local coroner concluded that the first child did die due to asphyxiation caused by strangulation, but a subsequent police investigation found that it happened accidentally, during rough play with another child his own age. The second child, it was determined, died as the result of a severe allergic reaction to a new asthma medication that only mimicked the signs of strangulation."

Jack stared at the text message without moving. After a few minutes he dialed Mike's number. The call wouldn't go through. He tapped the wall in horror, realizing that it was too thick to get a signal. He put the phone back into his pocket. Then he heard a low guttural laugh. It got louder and louder as it echoed through the small chamber. Jack frantically covered his ears with his hands to try to block out the awful noise. He pressed his palms against his ears harder hoping to dull the high pitched hysterical shrieking. It took him a very long time to realize that the sound was coming from inside his own throat.

✗

Marc Bilgrey has written short stories that have appeared in numerous anthologies and magazines. He is the author of two humorous fantasy novels, *And Don't Forget To Rescue The Princess*, as well as the next in the series, *And Don't Forget To Rescue The OTHER Princess*. Both are available as ebooks from Amazon Kindle.

His website is www.marcbilgrey.com

CRAFTY OLD BAGS

by Laird Long

The Crafts Connection and International Sisterhood of Tatters was an organization given over to the promotion and retail of crafts and spangled sweaterwear. Or so the promotional brochure claimed. The promotional brochure that lay crumpled in a dirty ball on the floor next to my size twelve body-holders. If you believed everything you read, you might as well return your brain for a refund and rent out the vacant space for *National Enquirer* back-issues storage. I live by the question mark and I'll die by the exclamation point.

Those thoughts, and other random images plundered from dog-eared skin mags, revolved through my steel-trap mind like Nietzsche's rolodex, as I packed my audit bag with various and sundry accounting and auditing weapons, and prepared to barge out the door for the one week audit of the above-mentioned guild. I checked my bag again: paper, calculator, pencils—mechanical and otherwise—hole-punch, stapler, file covers, jerky, bannock, pocket knife, Bible, brass-knuckles, etc., etc. …. Everything but an eraser and a drum of Wite-Out—those I wouldn't need. When I went out on an audit, the only time off I allowed myself was for bowel evacuation and the occasional recreational fist-fight.

Spud bellied up to my carrel that lay deep within the office maze. If he was expecting any cheese, he'd be cutting it himself. I held my breath. "Should be a fairly straightforward job, eh Clintsky? I'll handle the accounting work and you do the audit?" He rakishly waggled what he called a mustache and others called the world's smallest curling broom.

"Straightforward, huh?" I retorted.

"Aw, c'mon, Clint. Don't get started with all that—"

"What do we know about these crafters, Spud? What do we really know that they haven't told us? And if they haven't told us, what the hell are they hiding? And why? And for whom? And where? You see, Spud, the questions keep piling up like corpses at a CNIB rifle range. And where's it gonna end? Who's gonna stop it?"

Spud sighed, chewed his cud, blew the sediment off his glasses. "You?"

"No!" I yammered, and held up my concrete-cast fist. "Us," I challenged.

I was about to expound further on the benefits of audit teamwork, as Spud found a soft spot on the duct-taped carpet and prepared to grab a hearty handful of Z's, when Vanya tucked her streamlined physique into my airspace. She was leading the charge at the Crafts Connection.

"You guys coming?" she asked, sprinkling Spud and me with a double entendre as sticky as a pan-sized cinnamon bun.

"For you, sure," I said, stating the obvious.

"I gotta go to the can," Spud said, again with the obvious.

✗   ✗   ✗   ✗

I drove us the two downtown blocks to the Crafts Connection corporate head office. The log edifice had been hand-carved by a long-defunct tribe of one-armed chainsaw sculptors, and the morning gloom gave it a distinctly sinister cast. It squatted on a postage-stamp-sized lot amidst steel and glass skyscrapers, and glowered out at a pre-packaged, machine-manufactured world like a constipated senior on a poop chute. I kicked in the revolving door and ushered Spud and Vanya inside. Methuselah's sister greeted us from behind a Depression-era cash register.

"Are you folks from Twinkle & Winkle?" she crowed, a frowsy smile on her trembling, blue lips.

"Expecting someone else?" I queried roughly.

Vanya handled the small talk from there on in, and we set up our auditing operation in a renovated storage shed in back of the office-shop complex.

"Would anyone like some tea and Animal Crackers?" the old lady, whose name was Grace Goode, asked. She'd been peppering us with questions like we were strips of prime chuck ever since we'd elbowed into her set-up. She was the CEO, CFO, COO, and spokesmodel for the whole shebang.

"How about a tour of the dump, tomb raider?" I asked. Her lack of hearing kept the smile glued to her wrinkled face.

I translated my request into hand signals and she assented and showed us around the musty confines. The front part was the store—shelves and shelves of dolls, baskets, dried flower arrangements, wooden toys, and Boer-War-surplus armaments—while the back part held a meeting room, her office, and a lunch room that had been the kitchen set on "The Waltons." It was a cozy scene all right, with enough dried fruit to keep Truman Capote in clover, but my senses were sharpened to the cutting point by an odor other than potpourri in the air.

"You're not growing weed anywhere here, are you, Grandma Moses?" I asked. "You got a tea head to go with your bags?" I grabbed her lace collar and shook until her teeth rattled and rouge broke off her weathered face in glacier chunks.

"Oops! It's time to empty my colostomy bag," she bleated.

I let her go about her dirty business.

✗   ✗   ✗   ✗

Two days later and all clear. The audit was proving as dull as a CBC Canada Day special. Spud had scored a date with a sixty-year-old brooch, locket, and cameo saleswoman, but other than that the work had been proceeding with the monotonous regularity of a dumpster diver in back of a bran muffin plant.

"You taking the night shift?" Spud asked me, when Minnie Mouse spread her legs and showed six o'clock on his Disneyland watch.

"Yeah. I've still got some review notes I gotta clean up from my last two audits," I grumbled justifiably. Auditing, true auditing, was a process that could stretch on longer than Willie Horton's rap sheet.

Spud nodded, downed the final donut from his twenty-four case, and headed home.

I slammed a thick file down on the King James table and got to work. The file consisted of three pages of my audit work and forty-seven pages of review notes—queries and questions and requests for clarification from the senior and partner on the job.

The very idea of someone else questioning my work further curled my short 'n' curlies, but the stupidity of the questions and follow-up points is what really set the jelly in my brain to boil. "Why the profanity on page A2?" "Why the sketch of the Last Supper on page A3?" "What do you mean by: 'after popping Mr. Johnson in the groin, he confirmed that internal controls were as per the prior year'?" "After tracing fifty bills of lading to the shipping ledger, then to the unbilled revenue subledger, then to the billed receivables ledger, and then matching the receivables with the order input system printouts and the master logs, and the month-following cash receipts sub-subledger, why did you not trace back fifty sample items from the revenue masterfile to the bank reconciliation, to the cash receipts sub-subledger, and vice versa?"

My mind cocooned into a semi-comatose state as I flipped through the endless pages of nitpicking drivel. To say that some accountants were a little anal retentive was like saying a man wearing an industrial-sized butt-plug wasn't full of crap.

I was jolted out of my paper asphyxiation by the sound of sensible shoes clomping down the boardwalk hallway. Women who looked like they might've typed up the Ten Commandments on shale foolscap started trooping by my open door, headed for the meeting room. It wasn't their George Washington hairdos that threw me; it was their flagrantly Colombian features.

Grace creaked by, stopped, and informed me of what she wanted me to believe was going on. "A delegation of foreign tatters is in town, Clint, and we were just going to have a short meeting to discuss cross-cultural crocheting and frond-basket free trade. We'll try not to be too rowdy," she cackled, and shut the door on me.

I couldn't have swallowed her story if I'd been Linda Lovelace; it had all the integrity of a Soviet light bulb patent. I girded my loins, rose from the table, and pressed my ear to the paper mache wall that separated the office from the meeting room. Initially, all I heard was crinkling, crackling, and groaning—the ancient hoodlums seating themselves—but then the topic of cranky conversation quickly turned to drugs.

Ah-ha! I thought to no one but myself. I forged my thoughts into action and rattled the door of my cage. Locked! Grace's treachery surprised me no more than Walter Mondale's concession speech six months in advance of presidential election night—I'd found traces of Oil of Olay and Ben Gay amongst my audit papers the day after the first day of the audit. She'd been nosing around like an aardvark with a sinus problem. But if she thought for one frothy nanosecond that a locked door was going to stop me from exhuming her shenanigans, she, and the good people at Weiser, were sadly mistaken.

I turned the entry/exitway into wooden shrapnel with a pile-driving boot from my steel-toed brogan and charged down the hall and through the meeting room door. "Freeze!" I cried out.

It was a tableau right out of Dante's Inferno: eleven swarthy, hard-bitten South American biddies and Grace, the oldest unrestored structure in Western Canada, crowded around a doll-scattered boardroom table, tittering together as they planned their plans of world domination and clucking grotesquely as they assembled a visionary PERT chart that ended in the drug-polluted minds of a lost generation of tweens. I swallowed some righteous backflow, and, honestly, it tasted good.

"Did you have a question for me, Clint?" Grace asked, her parchment face as placid as a Death Valley dirt lake.

"*Si*," I glowered. "I wanna know what these dolls are made of?" I gestured at the ragamuffins lying about on the table. "Not sunshine and lollipops, I'll wager!?"

I trundled over to the table, casting aspersions right and left, mostly left, on the nation of Colombia as I advanced, and grabbed up one of the dolls. It looked like Queen Victoria as a full-grown child. I tore its widow-weeded head off and raised up its gruesome corpse like a primordial war club.

"Who wants to bet me that when I take a blowtorch to Barbie's great-great-grandmother here, she bleeds pure Colombian nose candy!? South American rock salt!" I turned my brimstone eyes on the nearest brown-betty who was dabbing at her nose with a wrist-mounted hanky. "Ever seen it snow in the tropics, Mother Earth!? Well, I have!"

My pulpit-thumping stirred the aged dope damsels to action, as I'd hoped it would.

Grace yelled something in Bogotá street Spanish that was probably, "Go, girls!", and a pack of wrinkly crime lords dove at me like the Canadian senior women's water polo team.

I tossed the decapitated doll aside, gave a battlefield roar, and got busy with my hands and feet. Two old crows met my fists in a love embrace and folded up like weathered barns in a dust-storm. A withered wench kicked me in the groin, but broke her rheumatoid toes on my steel-capped hockey jock. She wrenched her back by grabbing at her mangled mule, and I sent her puss an uppercut that started in the heated, underground parking garage and ended just above her wattle. Her wig cannonaded off her cadaverous skull and she straightened up like a graffiti artist at boot camp.

Blows started raining down on me like featherdusters, but the gnarled joy-toy grannies had seen a little too much of life and not near enough of death. I dispatched the last of the fantasy farmers with a knee to the dusty groin and faced Grace one-on-one.

"What a rude young man you are!" she swore, and then scooped up a fistful of humbugs and charged.

She threw the ball of candy at me and I let it bounce harmlessly off my scar-flecked faceplate. "Mandatory retirement time," I gritted through clenched teeth.

She sailed into me like she was the Titanic and I one-tenths of an iceberg. I squeezed the frail scarecrow to my Bunyan carcass in a crushing bearhug and heard her ribs snap like kindling in a petrified forest. She bit off a chunk of my ear and spat it in my face, a bilious smile cracking her fuzz-rimmed lips. She slumped into blessed unconsciousness before she could dine on my nose. I let her body crumple to the floor, and then wiped my feet on it. The stink of Henna was upon me, but my flared nostrils detected yet another odor—justice.

✗　✗　✗　✗

I stared at Vanya and Spud through the bars of my cell.

"Why'd you beat up all those old ladies?" Spud asked for the hundredth time.

I ignored his impertinence and shone my spotlights on Vanya. "When's Twinkle springing for the bail money!?" I shouted over the gruesome sound of some con finishing off his dinner with a visit to the galvanized Canadian Tire washroom pail behind me.

"When hell freezes over, is what he said," she replied.

I checked my mental calendar—November. "Another month then."

A cop built like a house, complete with a spacious veranda overhanging his belt, waddled into the sorry picture. "Yer free to go, Magnum," he said.

"Huh?" Spud asked.

"Yeah," the cop replied.

I brought the conversation out of the Stone Age by asking, "How come?"

"Revenue Canada jes' ruled that the dolls those crafty old bags were importing from Columbia aren't talkin' dolls, and, therefore, not political refugees with GST-exempt status, as defined in the Immigration Tax Act. It's gonna be hard time for Grace Goode—and probably eventual Canadian citizenship for those Colombian oldsters." The cop rubbed his fire-engine face in exhaustion.

"Huh?" Spud asked again.

"Yeah," the cop replied again.

As we strutted out into the ice-fogged dawn, I heard Vanya sigh, "You're lucky, Clint."

I snorted, showering Spud with my viscous contempt. "You don't want to be Goode to be lucky," I cracked.

✗

Laird Long: Big guy, sense of humor; pounds out fiction in all genres. Has appeared in many anthologies and mystery magazines and resides in Winnipeg, Canada.

THE PURLOINED PLATYPUS

A NERO WOLFE MYSTERY

by Marvin Kaye

At a few minutes after eleven that summer morning Wolfe entered the office and we exchanged our usual pleasantries, I told him that we'd had a call from Benjamin Moultrie.

He sat down in the chair reinforced to bear his seventh of a ton, rang for beer and then said, "That's a familiar name, but I don't remember why."

"He's president and board chairman of M–S–O–P."

"M–SOP? What on earth is that?"

"It stands for the Museum of the Strange, Odd and Peculiar. It's on the corner of 29th and Third Avenue."

"I've been mildly curious about that place," he said as he poured beer. "I've actually considered visiting it."

Wonder of wonders! I thought.

"So what does Mr. Moultrie want?" he asked.

"To be our next client." I knew it was unlikely, given the healthy condition of the bank account, but Wolfe said, "Ask him to be here tonight at nine."

I was surprised … but when I thought about it, I realized why Wolfe was in a good mood. Yesterday he'd received an invitation to visit his favorite orchid grower Lewis Hewitt at his estate on Long Island. That in itself wouldn't have made him so cheerful, for though he does enjoy visiting Hewitt, it still means enduring two long rides with white knuckles. But he'd been pestering his friend for years for a cutting of Hewitt's two rarest orchids and he finally said yes.

Before he changed his mind, I called Moultrie. He said he'd arrive promptly at nine.

⚹ ⚹ ⚹ ⚹

Good as his word, he rang on the hour sharp. I examined him through the peephole. He could have his picture in the dictionary under "Dandy." Middle-height with sleek black hair, he sported a trim mustache and a monocle. He wore a three-piece suit and tie; both looked expensive. Because it was a warm day in August, he had neither a topcoat or hat. I welcomed him and brought him to the office, buzzing Wolfe in the kitchen to cue his grand entrance. I had Moultrie sit in the red leather chair.

"Good evening," said Wolfe, entering and taking his seat. Fritz was right behind him with a pilsner glass and two bottles of Nordik Wolf beer, which I suspected he wanted to try because of its name. "As you see, sir, I am having beer. Would you care for a drink?"

"Thank you," the museum director said. "Either red wine or brandy would be appreciated." I told him what we had and he chose a snifter of Armagnac, which he sipped and proclaimed superb.

"I've been interested in your museum for some time," said Wolfe, as he sampled Nordik Wolf.

Moultrie smiled. "You must come as our guest. My grand-daughter Daphne says it's cool."

"I rarely leave the house, but I believe I will make an exception in this case. However, I do not think you are here because of the museum, are you?"

"Actually, Mr. Wolfe, I am. We've had a robbery."

"Oh? What was taken?"

"An extremely valuable platinum figurine in the form of a platypus. Its bill, feet and tail are gold and its eyes are two large diamonds."

"That sounds plenty valuable," I said.

"Yes. Its materials alone are worth a small fortune, but its ulti-mate value is historical. Though unconfirmed, it is believed to have been a gift from the Indian ruler of that time to none other than Kubla Khan. It was found at Xanadu, which was Kubla Khan's palace."

Wolfe finished his beer and tossed its cap in the drawer of his desk. He said to me, "By the way, Archie, this is superior."

"Glad to hear it. It's a shame they don't spell it with an E."

"Now don't be flippant." He opened the second bottle, poured, adjusted the bead, sipped and then returned to Benjamin Moultrie.

"Before I decide whether to take on your problem, you should know that my fee is large … some clients say exorbitant."

"I am aware of that. We are prepared to meet your price."

"When you say 'we' do you refer to other museum officers?"

Moultrie shook his head. "We do have a treasurer. His name is Michael Faraday. He operates out of his office at a Madison Avenue brokerage firm. But I wasn't counting him when I used the collective. I always include the museum itself."

Wolfe smiled. "I find that droll. Well, sir, what would you have me do? Find the missing figurine, or do you also wish me to apprehend the thief?"

"Both. It is likely that the culprit works for us."

"How many staff members do you employ?"

He held up one hand with all fingers raised. "Five. There's the cashier—"

"Please provide their names and details about them."

"Very well. Larry Winters is our cashier. He is a young man in his early thirties. Then there's the gift shop clerk, an attractive young woman, Linda Andelman. She and Larry are, as they say, 'an item.' The other three employees are security guards. They all wear uniforms with badges and caps. There's the daytime officer. His name is Mason Russell and he is, I believe, in his late fifties. He lives in Brooklyn with his wife. The night-time guard is Harold Johnson, a tall black man, unmarried, who lives in Greenwich Village. The last of the five is Marc Porterfield. He works the weekend shifts, day and night. He actually sleeps at the museum. Unmarried, very private. That's all I know about him except that he just had his forty-fifth birthday."

Wolfe finished his beer. "Mr. Moultrie, I have decided to take your case. My fee will be fifty thousand dollars, half payable before I begin. The second half, plus expenses, will be due when I have located the figurine and perhaps also identify the thief—but if I cannot do either, the fee still stands."

"That is acceptable." He took out his checkbook and pen and began to write. He proffered the check, which Wolfe read and passed to me. Then he said, "Archie, tomorrow I am going to cancel my morning session with the orchids. As soon as we finish breakfast, you will drive me to the museum, park and join me inside."

We arrived a little before 9:30. Parking wasn't a problem. I put it in a lot. The cost would be part of our expenses.

When I entered the museum and greeted Benjamin Moultrie, I saw Wolfe standing next to an attractive redhead, who was helping him browse through the gift shop. Every time it looked as if he might buy something, our client tried to give it to him as a gift, but Wolfe said no.

"Thank you, but this would not be a legitimate expense. If I choose to purchase anything, I will pay for it." He saw me. "Ah, Archie, you found a parking space."

"I put it in a lot."

He nodded. "Now let us begin."

Moultrie asked if he intended to interview his staff.

"Later. First, please show us the museum, including the spot where the figurine was before it was taken."

✗   ✗   ✗   ✗

There are six exhibit rooms, though Moultrie said he plans to open at least three more (insurrections, mutinies and revolutions; art, literature and music; U. S. presidential memorabilia). First he took us into a chamber filled with Egyptian artifacts such as statuary and vases; there were two mummies in their cases. "Those are authentic," our host said as he polished his monocle.

By contrast, the second room he guided us to was filled with comic book art, both American and foreign. I saw complete runs of *Action*, *Archie*, *Classic Comics* and its later incarnation, *Classics Illustrated*, *Donald Duck*, *Mad*, *Pogo*, *Spy Smasher*, *The Spirit*, *Star Wars* and various others. One large display case featured radio tie-ins such as *Captain Midnight* and *Little Orphan Annie* decoders, a *Tom Mix* Indian Arrowhead, *The Lone Ranger* western town, which, fully assembled, takes up a great deal of space. In one corner stood an array of figurines of Walt Disney characters: Daisy and Donald Duck, nephews Huey, Dewey and Louie, Goofy, Mickey and Minnie Mouse, Pluto, Uncle Scrooge and more.

I could have spent hours browsing and reading—Moultrie said all contents were on video so the originals needn't be handled.

Wolfe, however, was not interested and was ready to move on, so I promised myself to come back.

The third room was devoted to odd and often bizarre medical things. These greatly interested Wolfe, but he said, "I'd like to spend some time here, but for now let us see the other rooms." We passed briefly through a room devoted to the supernatural with exhibits of ghosts, ghouls, monsters, vampires, witches and wizards and were-things. Number five contained food and drink that would be right at home on Andrew Zimmern's Travel Channel shows *Bizarre Foods* and *Bizarre Foods America*.

When we entered the last room, which was devoted to Asian culture, Moultrie waved at an empty pad on a shelf inside a display case. "That's where the platypus was kept. The glass is quite thick; almost unbreakable." He opened his cell phone and showed us a photo of the platinum platypus.

"Archie," Wolfe asked, "is your phone capable of taking pictures?" I said yes. "Then see if you can copy the platypus from Mr. Moultrie." He waited till I did it, then turned to the museum officer and asked, "How many keys are there to this case?"

"Three. I have one set of all our keys and so does our treasurer. The third set is held by the senior security guard Mason Russell. He passes it to the night-time guard, who returns it to Mason each morning."

He nodded. "Mr. Moultrie, we will adjourn for lunch. When we return, I will want to speak to all available members of your staff. Perhaps you can arrange for the other guards to meet me at my office. Also Mr. Faraday. The sooner the better."

On our way out, he said, "Hopefully, our afternoon session won't take long and I'll be able to go up to the orchids at four. In the meantime, please prepare a camera. I want you to take photos in one of the rooms we've been to, also measurements."

"Which one? What pictures should I take and what measurements?"

He told me.

✗   ✗   ✗   ✗

I couldn't figure why he wanted pictures of a room that he showed no interest in, but when I got back I took them and then joined him just as he was about to question Larry Winters, the cashier. He's a young man with blue eyes and blond hair so light it's almost white. His suit was the kind of pastel hue you often see on houses in Hawaii. He said hello to me and shook my hand, then told Wolfe he hoped he could help him find the missing statuette.

"I notice that we are the only people in the museum," Wolfe remarked.

"We get busier in the afternoon."

Wolfe indicated the woman behind the counter in the gift shop. "I understand that you and Ms. Andelman are seeing one another."

Larry smiled. "Yes, we are. I've been saving money and working up the courage to propose to her."

I told him good luck.

"One more question," said Wolfe. "Do you have a set of museum keys?"

"No. Once in a while the night guard might ask me to pass them along to Mason, our day guard."

"Has that happened recently?"

He thought about it for a moment. "I don't think so."

But his sweetheart was close enough to hear him. "Larry," she said, "don't you remember? Harold gave them to you a few days ago to pass along to Mason, who got here late because the subway he takes got backed up."

Larry slapped his forehead. "That's right!" He turned to Wolfe. "I only had them briefly. Mason got here maybe five or ten minutes later."

"Very well," said Wolfe. "Now I have a few things to ask you, Ms. Andelman." He beckoned to Moultrie. "Do you have an office where I can talk to her and then Mr. Russell?"

Moultrie nodded. "I should have thought of that. Right this way." We followed him to his own headquarters, a modest-sized room with a mahogany desk and swivel chair, but before I shut the door he said to Wolfe, "I forgot to mention something. It might be important."

"I'm listening."

"About a week ago I received an offer to buy the platypus from the museum. It came from J. Nelson Barnett, an enormously wealthy art, curio and jewelry collector. He offered us one hundred thousand dollars. I almost took him up on it, but the platypus really belongs here."

"I see. If you have Mr. Barnett's address and other contact information, please give them to Archie."

"I'll have them for you when you come out."

He left and I shut the door. Wolfe invited Linda Andelman to sit down. There was no chair large enough for him, so he perched on the edge of Moultrie's desk.

"Ms. Andelman—"

"Please call me Linda."

"Very well. Linda, have you seen the missing figurine?"

"No, I never saw anything in the museum except for the gift shop and Mr. Moultrie's office."

"Never?!"

"It doesn't interest me. This is just a job, one I like, though."

Wolfe looked thoroughly minused (I'd taunted him once by using it instead of nonplussed). "I don't suppose," he said, "that you've ever been in possession of the museum's keys."

"That's right, I haven't."

"Do you get along with the rest of the staff? Obviously you do with Mr. Winters."

"Well, yes, he and I have been dating for a few months. I'm on a first-name basis with Mason and Hal—Harold, but I seldom run into Marc Porterfield and when I do, if I say hello, he just grunts. I mean he grunts in a mildly friendly way … I think."

"Thank you for your time," Wolfe said. "Could you ask Mr. Russell to come in here, please?"

She nodded and left. The daytime security guard arrived less than a minute later.

He wore a uniform with a cap that bore the initials M–S–O–P. What hair could be seen was salt-and-pepper black. He had an amiable smile and stood a little taller than me.

Wolfe gestured for him to sit down but he declined. "Thank you, but my uniform is a bit tight. I've been meaning to take it to my tailor for refitting."

"May I ask how long you have been a security guard for the museum?"

"From the first day it opened about nine years ago."

"Has there ever been a burglary before this one?"

"Never!"

Wolfe thoughtfully mulled it over, then said, "I have a hypothetical question. If you could steal anything in the museum and get away with it, what might it be?"

"That's an interesting question. It certainly would not be the platypus."

"Why not?"

"It would be nearly impossible to sell. The easiest way to turn a profit would surely be by taking complete runs of some of the comic books. The radio premiums would also be easy to get rid of on eBay."

Wolfe asked about his keys and then we were done.

✗ ✗ ✗ ✗

We got back just before four o'clock. Wolfe went up to the plant rooms, much, I'm sure, to Theodore's relief. Theodore, who is Wolfe's plant nurse, is convinced that all of the orchids will die if Wolfe misses a session.

I sat down at my desk just as the phone rang. It was Moultrie. He said both guards would be there at nine, thanks to Mason Russell, who agreed to stay for the night shift till Harold Johnson returned. Michael Faraday, the museum's treasurer, would also come at the same time. My instructions were that if he got there early I would show him to the front room, where he would wait till Wolfe finished questioning the security guards.

After he hung up I dialed the number he'd given me and I spoke with the collector J. Nelson Barnett. I asked him whether I could meet him the next day. When I told him why, he became quite cordial. "The platypus? By all means! Do you have my address?"

"Yes, I do."

"Then if you come at 11:30, I promise you won't have to wait. I'll tell my secretary to send you right in."

I thanked him, hung up and began catching up on the germination and blooming records. When Wolfe came down shortly after six, I reported my conversations with Moultrie and Barnett. It earned me a "Satisfactory."

✗ ✗ ✗ ✗

Faraday arrived at ten of nine. He is slim, trim and well-dressed. I estimated him to be in his early forties. I told him that he would have to wait for a while and led him to the front room. I offered him a drink and he asked if we had any single malt. When I said yes, he asked which ones. Answering took several seconds because we're well stocked with both single and blended scotch. He was delighted to learn that one of them is Edradour. "A brandy snifter, please," he said, then added, "Did you know it's the smallest distillery in Scotland?"

I said no.

"Of course it's been quite some time since I last visited Pitlochry, that's where they are, but when I did I found out that they only had two employees. There's also a rumor that Edradour is owned by the Mafia."

I brought him a snifter, napkin and the bottle so he might have a refill. He sat back contentedly with an expression that was positively beatific.

Just as I closed the door to the front room, the doorbell sounded and I saw that the two guards were there. Harold Johnson is quite tall with skin so light he could pass for Caucasian. He was in his MSOP uniform. Marc Porterfield wore a dark featureless suit, ditto tie. He nodded hello through spectacles so thick that I figured he has some kind of eye condition.

In the office, I offered libations and Johnson thanked me and asked for beer. The dour weekend guard went over to the bar and poured himself at least three ounces of Demerara rum, which made me shudder because it's 151 proof.

Wolfe entered and sat. Fritz brought him his usual two bottles of beer and one for Johnson. He had them on a tray so he could also manage two pilsner glasses. After thanking them for coming at such short notice, Wolfe repeated the same questions he'd put to Marc Russell. When asked what they'd steal from the museum, Hal, as he asked us to call him, agreed with Marc that the comic books would be the easiest to sell for a good profit. Porterfield, though, said he'd go into the medical room and help himself to some of the strange medicine there.

"Why?" Wolfe asked. "Would you sell them to a doctor or a hospital?"

"No, I don't need the money. I'd keep them."

"Are you talking about drugs? Narcotics?"

He shook his head. "Those might be salable, but I could be caught. No, I'm more interested in the poisons."

"For what reason?"

"Whatever." And that's all he would say.

Wolfe, exchanging a worried glance with me and Hal, decided to drop it. After I showed them out, but before I brought in Faraday, the boss beckoned to me. "We should find out about Mr. Porterfield."

"Why?"

"I've got a bad feeling about him. Call Saul later. Whatever he may find might need to be passed along to Inspector Cramer. Now let's see what Mr. Faraday has to tell us."

I brought him in. He almost shook Wolfe's hand but suddenly realized it was a bad idea. I told him to sit in the red leather chair, which he did. He immediately complimented Wolfe on the Edradour.

"Thank you, sir, but I seldom drink anything but beer and wine. The credit for stocking the bar belongs to Mr. Goodwin. I hope this visit isn't an inconvenience."

"Not at all. I've always wanted to meet you."

"May I ask why?"

"Two reasons. Orchids fascinate me and I should dearly love to see your collection."

"I will be delighted to do so after we talk. And why else have you wished to meet me?"

"I have a copy of your splendid cook book."

Wolfe chuckled. "Again, I do not deserve any credit. It was prepared by Ms. Barbara Burn, an editor at Viking Press. She, of course, spent a lot of time conferring with my chef, Mr. Fritz Brenner. But now let's get down to business. I presume that you are aware of the museum's theft?"

"Yes," he said with a sigh. "I've told Ben again and again that we must have plenty of insurance, but he only bought the bare minimum."

"Let me reassure you that the figurine will be found. Did you know that an offer has been made to buy it?"

"Oh, yes. I initiated it. Nelson Barnett is an old friend. I'm his financial advisor."

"Have you spoken to him since the theft?"

"I have," Faraday replied. "When he learned that Ben hired you to find it, he said it's the best thing he could have possibly done. He then told me, 'When—not if—it's found, I'll raise my offer to a quarter of a million.'"

Wolfe paused to open and pour his second bottle of Nordik Wolf. "I have one more question. Where do you keep your museum keys and how often do you use them?"

He took them out of his pocket. "They're always with me. I've never used them."

"Thank you for your time and assistance. Perhaps you'd like to have dinner with us sometime soon?"

"It would be an honor."

After he left, I called Saul and Wolfe picked up and told him what he wanted. What I heard made good sense.

✗   ✗   ✗   ✗

Next morning at 10:30 I introduced myself to Barnett's secretary, who showed me into his office and brought me coffee and a dimply smile. It was a large corner room on the 35th floor of a building at 47th and Madison. I sipped an excellent cup of Kona as J. Nelson Barnett entered. He wore a dark three-piece business suit and a necktie that I thought was black, but when he moved it caught the light and thin red slants glinted.

Barnett is so short I couldn't decide if he's a dwarf or a hobbit.

"Mr. Goodwin—"

"Just Archie."

"Archie, I'm glad you could meet me here, though I would have liked to visit Mr. Wolfe at his office."

"That could be arranged."

"Please be seated. Has the platypus been found?"

"Not yet," I said, "but Mr. Wolfe is confident that it will be. Why does it mean so much to you?"

"Well, I'm a collector, but I am *not* a hoarder. I feel that the platypus is too important historically for such a small, though excellent, museum. If I buy it, I plan to offer it to the Smithsonian."

"Did you have it stolen?"

He laughed. "No, Archie. But I know who did."

✗   ✗   ✗   ✗

When I reported later, Wolfe said, "It's just as I expected."

"Meaning?"

"It's show time. Or will be soon. Arrange a meeting, hopefully tonight at nine and ask Mr. Moultrie to come, also Messrs. Barnett, Faraday and Winters, as well as Ms. Andelman. And you might as well invite Faraday for dinner." Which shows that it's good to ask Wolfe to see his orchids.

"Might I suggest also inviting Barnett?"

He nodded. "I'll ask Fritz what we should serve."

I suggested braised platypus stuffed with crabmeat. He pretended not to hear me.

Dinner featured Beef Wellington, which Wolfe once said is a fine dish, "though it's not serious gastronomy." During the meal, he held forth on Dickens's final incomplete novel, *The Mystery of Edwin Drood*. "The problem," he contended, "is reasonably easy to solve if you are a competent detective. Have you read it?" Both guests said they had. "Good, then I won't ruin the experience for you. Here's what really happens and why." I excused myself and took my plate into the kitchen. I'd been meaning to read *Drood* and didn't want any spoilers.

✗   ✗   ✗   ✗

The museum director arrived promptly at nine along with his cashier and gift shop manager. They joined Wolfe and our guests in the office. Faraday relinquished the red chair to Moultrie. Drinks were distributed and Wolfe began.

"I was hired to find the platypus and identify the thief. It was soon apparent where the figurine was hidden, but I could not yet prove who took it."

"Never mind that for now," said Moultrie. "Where is it?"

Wolfe produced the photos I'd taken and passed them around. They all looked, but Moultrie said, "I don't see it!"

"That's because it's disguised. Tell me what you *do* see."

Moultrie stared with narrowed eyes. "It's some of the Disney statuettes."

"Yes. Which are most prominent?"

"Daisy and Donald Duck."

"Exactly. Can you tell me why I've asked you this?"

A bright light suddenly glowed in Moultrie's eyes. "Both of them have the same kind of bills as the platypus."

"That's right," said Wolfe. "Donald is the perfect camouflage. So you see, the platinum figure never left the museum. It should be there right now concealed behind Donald."

Barnett and Faraday both applauded. Wolfe nodded his appreciation, then continued. "Finding it is only half my job, though. Now I'll tell you who the thief is."

He looked pointedly at Larry Winters.

"Me?" he exclaimed. "Why me?"

"For two reasons," Wolfe answered. "First, there are only three sets of keys to the museum. One is held by your employer and the second by Mr. Faraday, who never uses them."

"How do you know that?"

"He told me so." He held up his hand to stop the next question. "Yes, I believe him. I asked my operative Saul Panzer to investigate both him and Mr. Barnett, also Ms. Andelman. They all have often been declared completely trustworthy. So you are the only one who had access to the platypus's display case."

"I told you I only had them for a few minutes."

"That's all it would take," Wolfe said. "Though you had longer. The day guard, who arrived late that day, says it was at least half an hour before he got to the museum."

"And what about the three guards?"

"I questioned them. None are even remotely interested in stealing it and for a good reason—it would be almost impossible to sell. Which brings me to my second reason. There is one person who wants to buy the platypus and he's sitting right here."

Winters looked at Barnett and sighed. "OK, you've got me. I offered it to him, but he refused. That's when I should have left town." All the while, I noticed that he was avoiding looking at Linda.

"Why did you want so much money?" Wolfe asked.

"So I could afford a house where Linda and I could live after we married."

She got up, approached him and slapped his face. Very hard.

✗   ✗   ✗   ✗

Of course Moultrie fired him, but said he would not turn him over to the police. "Furthermore," he said, "before you did this I was pleased with the excellence of your work. If you find employment elsewhere, I will give you a favorable letter of reference."

The cashier's jaw dropped, as did almost everyone else's. Not Wolfe, but I saw that our client's gesture made a great impression on him. "Mr. Moultrie," he said, "you are the soul of generosity. I am going to do something quite rare for me. With two conditions, you are released from paying the rest of my fee."

"Thank you! I agree to your conditions."

Wolfe waggled a finger. "You'd best hear them first. I want you to give the rest of my fee to the museum so that you can create the new rooms you told us about."

"Again, thank you! And what else?"

"Please allow me and Mr. Goodwin to visit at any time without charge."

"Done, sir. What about your expenses?"

"Archie will send you a bill for two parking lot costs and Mr. Panzer's fee, which, like mine, will be somewhat dear."

People began to rise to go to the front door (the cashier practically ran out).

But Faraday asked Wolfe if he could use the front room. When told that he could, he went in with Moultrie and Barnett. They were there for maybe two minutes. When they came back Moultrie said somewhat sadly, "I've decided to sell the platypus to Mr. Barnett."

✗   ✗   ✗   ✗

Two more things. When Wolfe found out what Saul learned about the weekend security guard, he had me call Cramer at once. It seems that though Porterfield was not married, he had been when he lived in Knoxville, Tennessee. His wife died soon after he took out insurance on her. Naturally he was suspected of killing her, but no one could figure out what did her in. The coroner put it down to the universal catch-all, heart failure. Cramer got in touch with the Tennessee police and worked out that she'd been given an almost undetectable poison. So the museum had to hire a new weekend guard.

Lastly—and this may have been a joke on me, though that's not Wolfe's style—I actually overheard him asking Fritz whether he thought an acceptable meal could be prepared with platypus meat.

But so far, I have not tasted any.

⚔

Marvin Kaye is the author of seventeen novels and numerous short stories, as well as the editor of *Sherlock Holmes Mystery Magazine*, *Weird Tales* magazine, and many best-selling anthologies. A native of Philadelphia, he is a graduate of Penn State, with an M.A. in theatre and English literature.

221B

by Vincent Starrett

Here dwell together still two men of note
Who never lived and so can never die:
How very near they seem, yet how remote
That age before the world went all awry.
But still the game's afoot for those with ears
Attuned to catch the distant view-halloo:
England is England yet, for all our fears--
Only those things the heart believes are true.
A yellow fog swirls past the window-pane
As night descends upon this fabled street:
A lonely hansom splashes through the rain,
The ghostly gas lamps fail at twenty feet.
Here, though the world explode, these two survive,
And it is always eighteen ninety-five.

A RUDE AWAKENING

by Stan Trybulski

Kozhevnikov came out of the Metro at the Place du Colonel Fabien station and trudged slowly down the Boulevard de La Villette. The late afternoon April sun was bright in his face but not strong enough to take the chill out of the air. He tightened the wool scarf around his neck and turned up the collar of his pea jacket. Standing at the corner of the Rue Burneuf, he paused and then turned into that street and started a slow climb up the hill. The climb was steep and even though Kozhevnikov was a pudgy man with short, squat legs he did not find it difficult after years of cross country skiing in the hills outside Moscow. It was just that it was, well, a boring walk past boring houses on a boring street. A boring oblique path to another of the boring routine tasks he had been given since his arrival in Paris four months ago.

When he reached the Avenue Mathurin, he crossed and turned downhill, returning to his starting point, the Place du Colonel Fabien, but from the opposite side. On the other side of the Avenue was the French Party headquarters: six stories of sinuous glass, guarded by a squat, semicircular domed structure almost shoved into the ground as if it were some sort of slapdash futuristic military bunker. The dome covered the French Party's subterranean conference center.

Kozhevnikov shrugged. An underground hideout was more like it. It fit their clandestine mentality, a holdover from the Great Patriotic War. Now the French comrades were in a retreat, in fact you could call it a rout, but they were too stubborn to take our advice. What is one to do with them? Oh, they listened to us all right, but then they just went ahead and did things their own way.

Officially, he was a Soviet liaison to the trade unions and one of his tasks was to travel out to Poissy and meet with selected union leaders at the sprawling Peugeot car works. The shop stewards were Party members and politely listened when he would encourage them to support the brave Nicaraguan and Salvadorian comrades fighting the American imperialists. But when it came to talking about the plant and its production techniques and design, they were as animated as any of their big capitalist bosses. He had to confess he was as enthusiastic as they were for he had studied automotive technology back in Moscow. But when he included the technical comments in his first reports, Comrade Grubkin, the Embassy's second secretary, head of the KGB *residentura* and his Service boss, crossed them out and insisted that the reports be re-written with more "information" about French worker support for the struggle of the oppressed peoples of Central America against American imperialism.

"Filip, you must pay stricter attention to what Moscow wants," Grubkin said. "Paris is a cushy job; be glad you're not in Afghanistan, surrounded by Abduls looking to slice your nuts off."

He had followed Grubkin's advice and it had paid off. A month earlier Grubkin had called him into his office and greeted him with a broad smile. "I know your formal training was cut short and that you never received the full syllabus of case studies, but I have a task for you that perhaps is the best way to develop you as a street-man."

Grubkin assigned Kozhevnikov what he called "important work for the Service" and a "sensitive task" involving the French comrades. He knew enough not to comment but only listen and did not even smile when Grubkin told him there would be an increase in his field allowance for the duration of the task. When Grubkin reminded him that, of course, all expenditures would have to be accounted for, Kozhevnikov solemnly nodded agreement. He had grown up poor and his only luxury had been a pair of handcrafted Norwegian cross-country skis that he had bought at a flea market. Now in Paris he was still poor and the skis were still in Moscow. So if he could only have a beer or two on the Service, he would not complain. And this day, that was exactly what he intended to do.

He stopped and looked at his watch. Thirty minutes early. Good, he told himself, I *will* have *two* beers. He casually walked the perimeter of the Place until he reached a small café situated directly across from the French Party headquarters. People were sitting on the café's tiny terrace, having a beer or a glass of wine and chatting. Kozhevnikov could tell that they were workers and would have loved to have joined them, to have a conversation about … what? He was unsure how to develop an unstructured chat. With the auto workers, he had always talked from a Moscow-approved script.

Instead, he went inside the café and sat by the window where he had a clear view of the Party building. The barman came over and Kozhevnikov ordered a large Stella Artois, while keeping his eyes on the street. This was the fifth time that he had conducted this task and had decided that it actually was important Party work. For on the first surveillance, he had seen a ZIL limousine from the Embassy pull up in front of the French Party headquarters and the First Secretary emerge from the building and get in the back.

Twenty minutes later, his target emerged: Dubos, a thin man of medium height, dressed in a dark blue suit with white shirt and black tie. Kozhevnikov hurriedly paid the barman and followed Dubos to an apartment block a few streets away. His target came out two hours later with a young woman whose long blond tresses fell onto a cashmere jacket that covered a cashmere sweater. The couple walked arm in arm down the hill and across the Canal St. Martin to the Place de la Republique and then to a restaurant on small street just off the Boulevard Voltaire. He waited on the corner until they had finished eating and then followed them back to the woman's apartment building.

When they went inside, Kozhevnikov hurried back to the restaurant and asked to see the menu. Duck breast with honey and rabbit in mustard sauce were the specialties of the evening. How bourgeois a meal for a comrade. Yet how wonderful. He sighed, thinking of the simple meal of sausage, potatoes, and cabbage he would prepare for himself later that evening.

His report to Comrade Grubkin included a description of the woman and the name of the restaurant and its specialties, even though he felt such details might cast an unwarranted aspersion on the French comrade.

"Very good, Filip," Grubkin had said. "Always keep the report short. We don't want to overtax any Moscow brains. Yet make it interesting so that the Center asks for more." The next three surveillances of Dubos were the same. He arrived at the café at the set time, nursed a single beer and watched as the Embassy car pulled up in front of the French Party headquarters, watched the First Secretary emerge from the building, get in the car and drive off. Then almost twenty minutes later, Dubos would leave and he would follow him to the same apartment block and wait until he emerged with the blonde.

When he would follow them downhill to the *resto*, he wished the streets were full of snow and pushed his legs forward as if he were on his cross-country skis, and while he waited for them to finish their meal he dreamed of snowy hills and remembered the pictures he had seen of posh ski resorts in the Alps. He knew that downhill skiing was merely an outdoor entertainment of the rich, capitalist ruling classes. Still he would liked to have tried it, feeling the rush of the ice-cold wind across his face as he zigzagged across a glacier face; to have a cup of chocolate with brandy and whipped cream while he looked out over a long range of snow-capped peaks; and to have that duck breast with honey and a whole bottle of a good red wine. And with a young blond woman sitting across from him, smiling a smile that was as delicious as the meal and meant only for his eyes and heart.

Now that was the kind of dream the Service was on the lookout for. A dangerous, stupidly romantic dream that if known would mean his immediate recall to Moscow. He left it quickly and returned to his surveillance. There was no doubt in his mind that the appearance of the First Secretary at the French party headquarters and the surveillance of the target were connected.

"Coincidences do not exist in our line of work. Always remember that, comrades," the instructor back in Moscow had told them their first day in school.

The barman brought the beer and he took a long sip, first of the foam, then of the liquid, letting the sharp, cold carbonation pop on his tongue and sting it before swallowing. He would have loved to have a glass of red wine; it was far better here than in Moscow, where you could only get swill from Georgia or Bulgaria, Hungary if you were lucky. But that would be an expense too much.

Still he had much to be thankful for. Only last year his intended destiny was some outdated and freezing automotive plant. Now he was in Paris, with a warm flat, larger than the one he had shared with his mother, and even though the flat was outside Paris, in Montrouge, where the Party controlled the government, to him it was the same. And even though a glass of good wine was too dear an expense, he was able to buy fresh vegetables and plenty of meat, even though it was the cheaper cuts.

His life had changed the year before as he waited at the tram stop by the university. A man approached, a nondescript face with nondescript clothes and a soft voice. A soft voice was all he needed with Kozhevnikov for his Service shield spoke for him. The man took him to a nearby café where he bought him a beer and explained that the Service was in need of young graduates with Kozhevnikov's talents. When he appeared puzzled, the man mentioned his ability to understand automotive technical literature printed in English, French, and German. He had sense enough not to ask how the Service knew that. As far he was concerned, they were an omniscient deity. And when he was invited to start training for intelligence work with them, he knew it wasn't really an invitation, for if he declined he would become suspect and would be lucky if he found a technical job in Chelyabinsk, let alone Moscow.

So he went along. It was to be two years of training, but after only eight months it was suddenly cut short and he was ordered abroad.

"*Do you have dreams?*" a Service psychiatrist asked him just before he was posted to Paris. "*Tell me about them,*" the doctor continued, knowing that, of course, Kozhevnikov, like everyone else, had dreams. When he hesitated, the doctor intoned, as if he had the speech memorized: "*Your dreams, like everything else, now belong to the Party and the Organs of the State. We will know them sooner or later, so it is better if you tell us now so we can decide your fitness to do important work.*"

I dream of the snow, he answered.

"*Well, this is winter in Moscow and that is to be expected. What about recurring dreams?*"

I dream of the day that Marxism-Leninism triumphs over imperialism, he said.

The doctor casually wrote down the answer, as if he had heard it a hundred times before. Which Kozhevnikov was sure the man had.

To have a decent red wine and have the Service pay for it, now that was another dream. He laughed silently at the thought. He had not told the doctor that, nor had he told the doctor that his dream about snow included a cross-country ski trip that took him all the way to the Finnish border.

Even though he always limited himself to one beer each time he was at the café, the surveillance task had turned out to be rather enjoyable. He saw many of the same customers and while he never conversed with any of them, now by this fifth time here he felt he was blending in. Perhaps he should mention this to Grubkin, maybe it would lead to further such assignments. He mulled that idea over while he finished his beer, not coming to any conclusion.

The door opened and a blond woman came in and hugged a young man standing at the end of the bar. Kozhevnikov had seen her the last time he had been here and found her quite attractive, unlike the girls back in Moscow, who if attractive either attached themselves to powerful men or became nightclub whores. This woman, her arm around the man who was obviously a worker like himself, joked with him and the barman, giving an infectious laugh that floated across the room. She was more beautiful than any woman he had ever seen in Moscow, yet she did not seek out the powerful or look to sell her body to the highest bidder. She was perfectly happy drinking a glass of red wine in a working-class bar with other workers. This realization made Kozhevnikov happy and sad at the same time.

He watched her reflection in the window, tossing her blond hair as she laughed and joked. He also looked at his own face, square, almost brutish with its smashed-in nose, a present he received at the age of thirteen from his drunken father who came home to find his mother out and only young Filip to bash around. His father was a Party member who did his job and bought drinks for his superiors instead of buying food for his family, and so nothing was ever done about it. The next winter the old man passed out drunk in a park where Filip was sure he had gone in search some cheap whore. When the maintenance workers found him the next morning, he was frozen to death.

As the son of a deceased Party member in good standing, Filip was able to study automotive technology with an eye to a future as … as what? He turned and looked directly at the woman. She seemed to notice and smile at him. He blushed and turned back to the window and peered at his face. If he could ever get the nose fixed, he decided, he would not look half bad, and perhaps attract someone better than chunky farm girl Iliana, the only woman at the Embassy who paid him any attention, but whose appearance was more fit for driving a tractor at a collective than working in the Paris Embassy.

The barman handed her a small metal *jeton* for the phone. She stood and started walking back towards him. As she passed the entrance, the door opened and a small man with wire-rimmed glasses entered. He too looked at the woman. As she passed Kozhevnikov, the aisle so narrow she could barely squeeze through, he felt her hand brush along his shoulder, almost squeezing it, as if he was an old friend. He closed his eyes at the sudden thrill that ran through him and when he opened them again, the small man with the wire-rimmed glasses was sitting across from him.

"Do you mind?" the man asked in a quiet voice. "This seems the only seat available."

He shook his head in the negative and started to look back out the window.

"She's very beautiful, isn't she?" The voice drifted soothingly into his ears.

Kozhevnikov suddenly turned to him in surprise. "Who?"

The Quiet Man nodded in the direction that the blonde had gone, to the telephone *cabinet*.

"Oh, yes, her, she is very beautiful." He answered as the Quiet Man's voice still hung in the air. The man's French was colloquial, like the other patrons, yet his demeanor, the tone of his voice, even his eyeglasses indicated that he was something else. And it appeared as if he did not care who knew it.

"She is coming back."

Kozhevnikov felt a cool hand on his shoulder as the blonde squeezed past.

"*Excusez-moi, monsieur*," she said, leaning slightly against him. The smile was still on her face and it mesmerized Kozhevnikov. He could barely nod a reply and kept watching as she joined her companion at the end of the bar. When he turned his attention back to the café window and the entrance to the French party headquarters across the way, his gaze swept past the Quiet Man who was busy wiping his glasses on his sweater.

"You missed your man, comrade. How will you explain it?" The Quiet Man's voice was so soft that Kozhevnikov thought for a split second that he had misheard him. But only for a split second.

"I don't know what you mean. And why do call me comrade?"

The Quiet Man smiled. "We are all comrades of a sort, and yes, you do know what I mean. You know very well what I mean."

Kozhevnikov started to rise, to hurry out of the café and chase after his target.

"Sit," the Quiet Man said. "You cannot catch up to him." The voice was just above a whisper, but something in it caused Kozhevnikov to slump back down into his chair. He watched as the Quiet Man signaled to the barman, holding his fingers up like the way Churchill made a V. The barman brought two glasses of red wine to the table.

"Go ahead, try this, it's a decent Côte du Rhône."

Kozhevnikov did not touch his glass. He sat there, silently watching as the Quiet Man sipped his wine. After swallowing, the man set his glass down and placed the tips of his index fingers on a pair of pursed lips and stared at Kozhevnikov.

Anger and fear simultaneously welled up in Kozhevnikov. "Just who are you?" He tried to put importance in his voice.

"As I said, a comrade."

"I have not seen you at the Embassy. Have you been sent from Moscow?" His voice had lost its tone of importance.

The Quiet Man removed the tips of his index fingers from his mouth and set his lips into a wry smile. "Moscow? No, and you should thank your lucky red stars that I have not been."

Kozhevnikov's eyes widened and as if sensing his thoughts, the Quiet Man shook his head. "You can run if you want to. We won't stop you. But you know it will go badly for you back at the Embassy, behind those high walls and electronic doors and the cameras watching every corridor, every entrance and every exit, and the thugs ever anxious to do whatever the Service, your Service, deems necessary in cases like yours …." His soft voice drifted off and he sipped some more of his wine. "Your superior will be on the backchannel to Moscow Center before you can utter your first syllable of explanation. And no matter what you tell them," the Quiet Man's voice was suddenly firmer, "it will end very badly for you. You know their feelings on matters like this, their suspicions, their methods. No matter what you tell them, they will demand more, for they always believe there is more. And they would be right, wouldn't they? *We* always have something to hide."

He gestured at Kozhevnikov with the wine glass. "And so they will ship you back to Moscow in the morning … maybe even tonight … and let the experts deal with you."

Kozhevnikov slumped back in his chair. He knew the Quiet Man was right and he could see that the Quiet Man knew that he knew. "What do you want from me?" His voice sounded tired.

"It's rather stuffy in here. Finish your drink and we can go outside where the air is bracing and walk."

"A walk? Where?" Kozhevnikov still had not touched his wine.

The Quiet Man smiled. "Not far. And don't worry about your target. We can take you to him after we're done. It will be as if you had always been thirty meters behind him."

Kozhevnikov seized his wine glass and quickly drank the entire contents, ignoring the grimace on the Quiet Man's face.

Outside, the Quiet Man buttoned up his coat. "I'm sorry, I fear I have been rather impolite; allow me to introduce myself. I am Mr. Cuthwick." He held out his hand.

Kozhevnikov did not take it. Cuthwick? The man must be British and to Moscow the British imperialists were as bad as the Americans, only more feeble.

"Well then, we might walk this way," the Quiet Man said, gesturing at the length of the La Villette. He started walking and Kozhevnikov followed. *Might*? The British snobs and their bloody subjunctives; they turned the English language unto something even more difficult than the French. At least we're walking downhill, he silently concluded. As they walked, glum thoughts still crowded his mind and he did not notice that the young man who had been chatting up the blonde in the café was now right behind him.

The Quiet Man stopped when he was parallel with a gray Citroën sedan, one of a million in the Paris region. The young man suddenly came up and unlocked the front door on the passenger side, then reached around and popped up the lock on the back door. The Quiet Man opened it and gestured to Kozhevnikov to get in. After he did, the Quiet Man slid in beside him and the young man opened the driver's side door and sat behind the wheel.

"Where to, sir?" He was speaking to the Quiet Man while watching Kozhevnikov in the rear view mirror.

"Oh, here and there, nowhere in particular, I'm just going to have a chat with our new friend." He withdrew a fancy cigarette case made of onyx and silver that flashed as they approached and passed a street light. He opened it and offered one to Kozhevnikov. "Go ahead, they're not drugged; they're perfectly safe, if you're not afraid of cancer. American, with filters." He took one himself and lit it.

Kozhevnikov waved the case away. "You said you wanted to talk. What about?"

"Automobiles. We work for a large automobile importing firm." He drew on his cigarette then rolled down the window a crack and exhaled. "We are looking at the possibility of importing Russian cars."

"And just where will you import them?"

"All over. We have an international clientele, quite distinguished firms." The Quiet Man stared at him. "But this could only come about if they are worthwhile."

"Why come to me? You should speak with the manufacturers in Moscow." Kozhevnikov asked the question although he already knew the answer.

"Because they might not give us straight answers and because you have a good knowledge of Soviet automobile engineering."

I knew it. Kozhevnikov followed this silent conclusion with a dozen silent curses. The Soviet Embassy is a sieve. How would Comrade Grubkin like to hear that? He cursed again when he realized he could never tell him.

"Now take your limousines," the Quiet Man continued. "Solid, well-built from all appearances. The ZIL 4014, for instance. That might very well suit a wide array of our customers." He puffed again on his cigarette and exhaled. "We would like an independent opinion … from you. And, of course, we would pay for your advice."

Kozhevnikov suddenly felt relieved. There could be no harm in confirming what was already public information. "What exactly are you looking for?" He managed to keep his voice even, regarding that as a minor triumph.

"The ZIL 4014 floor plan. Can you sketch it out for is?"

"Of course, but …." Kozhevnikov was about to add that they could find it in any Russian automotive journal but suddenly realized that if he told them that, they might want something else, something more difficult.

"But what, comrade?" The Quiet Man's voice softly floated in the air.

"The sketch would be rough, not draftsman's standards."

The Quiet Man reached into the breast pocket of his coat and produced a piece of white paper and a pen. "Could you do it here? Now?"

"Yes, if you really want it tonight."

The Quiet Man raised his voice to the driver. "Find a spot and pull over, even if it's illegal. We'll only be a moment."

After the car stopped, Kozhevnikov quickly sketched the floor plan and handed it over.

The Quiet Man peered at it. "Now, can you show us on the sketch how you would armor the ZIL? Where, what type of armor and how thick, and what you think the new weight might be?"

Kozhevnikov took back the paper and started working. When he was done, he handed the paper to the Quiet Man, who quickly glanced at it before stuffing it in his coat pocket, his hand returning with a small envelope. "Go ahead, open it."

Taking the envelope, Kozhevnikov opened it and counted out $1000 in American hundred-dollar bills. "Thank you," was all he could say.

"Righto," the Quiet Man said to the driver, "let's get to the restaurant. Our friend has a target to follow." He turned to Kozhevnikov. "You will be pleased to know that your man followed his usual routine with his mistress. You can pick up your surveillance at the restaurant."

"Is that all you need from me?" Kozhevnikov gestured toward the Quiet Man's coat pocket where the sketch was safely stashed. His voice was firm, the worry banished to some cerebral Siberia.

The Quiet Man sighed. "Well, there is one more thing."

"What?" Suddenly Kozhevnikov was worried again.

"Dubos. The man you have under surveillance."

"What about him?"

"Well, you see, we are interested in him, too."

"You want me to report to you, as well?" Kozhevnikov's words were laced with anger.

"No, not in the least, we would never ask that of you." The Quiet Man smiled.

"What then?" Kozhevnikov was puzzled.

"Simply put, there will be times when we don't want you to watch him, but to file your usual report as if you had."

"I will not! Here, take your goddamned money back." Kozhevnikov threw the envelope onto the Quiet Man's lap. His face was flushed with rage and embarrassment that this little imperialist swine could think that he could be so easily compromised.

"Yes, you will." The Quiet Man's voice was no longer soft. It was time for the cake or death approach, to present this flabby man with the only two choices available to him. "For if you don't, the sketch you drew, showing how the ZIL limousine your Party leaders use is armored, will find its way to Comrade Grubkin. Yes, we know all about Grubkin. And along with the sketch will be this little envelope with the American money. And then there will be the anonymous call to Grubkin from 'a friend,' asking if he has examined the sketch and money for fingerprints." The Quiet Man leaned forward and spoke to the driver. "What do you think our new friend's breaktime will be, Geoffrey?"

The driver laughed. "Oh, I'd say no more than five hours. If they flutter him first, then three hours should do. Not even enough time for the Lubyanka hoods to enjoy themselves."

The Quiet Man named Cuthwick turned back to Kozhevnikov. "So that is why you will do this favor for us. And when you do, we will give you back the sketch and the envelope, which will have much more money it."

"Keep your goddamned money." Kozhevnikov's voice was still filled with rage, but this time it was the rage of the defeated.

✗   ✗   ✗   ✗

After he finished typing his report he was too tired, too afraid, and too sick at heart to get up and bring the piece of paper to Grubkin. He placed the report in a manila envelope, sealed it with the "eyes only" security tape and took it over to the typists' pool. "Good morning, comrade," he said, smiling at Iliana. "I am working on something important and it would be a favor to me if you could take this report to Comrade Grubkin and place it in his in-box."

"Of course, Filip. It would be my pleasure." She smiled back at him and took the envelope, touching his hand with hers. He entrusted her with this task of office courier because not only did she so obviously like him but because she actually was not a typist, but the gate keeper to the *residentura's* strong room. Thus, after transmission to Moscow Center, the report would eventually come to her to be locked away.

Back at his desk he sat there frozen, his head in his hands, unable to think coherently. What had he done? Grubkin was sure to find something suspicious about the report, despite the promises of the Quiet Man that everything would appear normal. He should have stayed in Moscow, gone to work in the auto factory, even designing trucks that would never run properly would have been better than this. But simultaneously with that thought came rushing the realization that the choice had never been his. When the Party comes knocking at your soul, you must always be home to welcome them. He continued to sit there, unmoving, frozen in terror.

"Does your head hurt, Filip?" Iliana's voice suddenly shocked him. He took his hands away from his face and looked up to see her standing there, holding the sealed manila envelope, a look of concern on her face. The terror inside him increased as she thrust the envelope at him. "Comrade Grubkin said to tell you it was a decent job but to take a look at the notes he wrote in the margin before I lock it up."

Suddenly all the terror he had felt floated away and he smiled at the woman. He took the envelope and thanked her. When she did not turn and leave he asked, "Yes, comrade?"

"Your head, does it hurt? Are you ill?"

He drew deep breath. "Oh, no, it is nothing, I was just trying to puzzle out that important assignment I told you I am working on." When she left, he closed his eyes and placed his hands back on his face. He breathed slowly, calming his racing heart which was now leaping for joy instead of constricting in fear. It was going to be fine, he knew. All he had to do was think everything through carefully and do what the Quiet Man wanted.

✗   ✗   ✗   ✗

The next meeting with the Quiet Man was at a small bookshop, not even a *librairie*, really nothing more than a bookstall with cases filled randomly with used books, many of them about art. The bookshop was deep in Montparnasse, just off of the Rue d'Alésia and not far from his flat. If Kozhevnikov saw the Quiet Man holding a copy of *Finnegan's Wake*, then it would be safe. He arrived early and only found the proprietor, an old lady with gray hair tied in a bun and wearing a drab black sweater over a faded print dress. She was sitting on a wooden chair next to a table half-filled with books, its empty space serving as her counter. There was no cash register, all proceeds immediately disappearing into one of the pockets of the sweater, only to later reappear in some jar in the woman's kitchen. There would be no money here to help stock the Elysée Palace's sumptuous wine cellar.

He smiled at the thought and greeted her with a slight nod, avoiding a pair of cold gray eyes, and began rummaging through the stacks as if he were really in the mood to buy something.

He stopped in front a shelf of art books and was scanning the titles when his eyes fell upon the cover of a large folio with a black and white ink drawing of a strange machine on its cover. The machine had pistons and cams, wheels and rotors, fan belts and an engine, all attached by lines that continued on and ended in mid-air. The engine was at the top of the contraption and decorated with a star. Around the star was a sickle, fashioned into part of a fan belt that moved a series of cogs. In the middle of the contraption were another star and another sickle-belt that turned nothing.

Kozhevnikov was fascinated. Who was the comrade who drew this? Everything was so irrational and yet all connected. Had the artist been hallucinating? He opened the dust jacket and looked at the inside of its front. A legend in bold script announced in English that the cover art was *"The Roaring of Ferocious Soldiers,"* by Max Ernst, 1919. 1919? He knew from his study of the Party's history and the workers' movement that the German proletariat had attempted a revolution that year. Was this Ernst a Communist? Why had he never heard of him?

He began leafing through the folio and found another Ernst drawing, this one of a machine built upon a tractor tread. On top of this machine, whose purpose he could not discern, was a star inside another star, unattached to the machine, floating in mid-air. How strange, he thought, it is so much like me, floating unattached yet near a machine whose real purpose I also cannot fathom.

Kozhevnikov turned the pages. There were drawings and paintings of machines and autos by French and Italian artists that also fascinated him. He was particularly intrigued by more strange contraptions. This time they were not pen and ink drawings like those of Ernst but photographs of things that had been actually built. The artist was Marcel Duchamp. Duchamp? Well, at least he knew of Duchamp. The artist who had given up his art to play chess. How Russian that was, he thought.

At another section in the book, he stopped and stared at the names. Tatlin, Goncharova, Malevich, El Lissitzky, Popova, Vesnin. They were Russians and again he had never heard of them, had never before seen their work. Why? Had they been traitors? Anti-Soviets? His mind whirled with sudden thoughts. Even if they had been traitors, their work was wonderful, and did it not belong to the Russian people? There but for the grace of The Party could have been me. But only if I lived somewhere else, if I was somebody else.

He was stunned by his own thoughts but forced his fingers to continue turning the pages. He stopped again when he saw a drawing of a machine that had a large fan, like the ones that cooled the engines of the ZIL limousines. Underneath two of the horizontal fan blades were penned the words: "*A L'Ombre D'Un Boche.*" The artist was Francis Picabia. The folio had many more drawing by Picabia and Kozhevnikov was enamoured by them, as well. Was the artist also a comrade, an anti-fascist? Kozhevnikov suddenly realized that he didn't care. Francis Picabia was such a beautiful name. Every fiber of his being now wanted to make it his and he closed the book. He stood there, silently mouthing "I am Francis Picabia" over and over, until he knew that he must make it true, go far, far away, as far away from Moscow as possible, to the mountains of Peru, maybe the beaches of Mexico. Change his name to Picabia and change his life. He could draw, only technical drawing to be correct, but perhaps he could also become an artist, really become Picabia.

The narrow aisle between the stacks was lit by a dim solitary fluorescent bulb hanging from the ceiling. It flickered like a candle, casting strange shadows over the rows of books. It was quiet as he stood there, head bowed, clutching the folio as if it were the Bible, silently mouthing his litany like one of the reactionary Orthodox prayers that he had heard his grandmother say. The only sound was the occasional soft scrape of the chair in the front of the store.

A creak of the floorboards interrupted his concentration and he raised his head. At the back of the shop, near the end of the aisle, there was a small, humped mass. The Quiet Man had arrived early and was holding the James Joyce book in his hand. It was safe to approach. So why wait for the appointed time? Still clutching the folio, Kozhevnikov eased down the aisle. When he reached the Quiet Man, he touched his shoulder and announced, "Hello."

His contact turned and smiled. The smile disappeared when he saw the shock on Kozhevnikov's face.

"I'm sorry," Kozhevnikov stammered at the strange face. "I thought you were someone else."

"I am Picabia," the man announced.

"No, you cannot be," Kozhevnikov said. "I am Picabia. I am Picabia. I must be Picabia! I will become Picabia," he was shouting now, angry at this little man trying to steal his new identity. "And I will live in the mountains of Peru! Or live on the beach in Mexico!"

The chair in the front of the shop scraped against the floor again; this time loudly, with a sense of urgency. He could hear the patter of feet on the creaking floorboards and the old woman's breath on his neck.

"Don't touch me, I am Picabia!" he shouted again. Then he shoved the not-Picabia with both of his hands. The man did not move. He shoved him again but he still stood his ground in the narrow aisle. Everything was whirling in his mind, it was going all wrong. He kept shoving the man but the man would not move.

He suddenly felt a hand seize his shoulder and shake it. A soft hand, cool like the one the blond woman in the café had touched him with.

"Filip! Wake up, wake up!"

Why was she so rude? He opened his eyes and looked around. He was at his desk and Iliana the typist was staring at him with her silly cow eyes.

"Are you feeling ill?"

Before he could answer, he saw Grubkin hurrying toward them. "What is going on?" Grubkin asked.

Kozhevnikov could only stammer out, "I … I don't know what happened."

Grubkin turned to Iliana. "Well, comrade?"

"I heard him yelling and when I came over to his desk, I saw that he was asleep and I shook him awake. That is all."

"That is not all, comrade. What was he yelling?"

"Something about he was Picabia, not somebody else. Or was it?" She was suddenly confused.

Grubkin's face screwed up into a deep frown. "Picabia?"

"Yes, comrade. And he was going to live in the mountains of Peru or maybe on the beach in Mexico. It was confusing. But who is Picabia? Is it an operational name?"

"Never mind." Grubkin walked over to the wall and pressed a red button. A few seconds later two security officers appeared at the door and Grubkin waved to them.

"Is this necessary, comrade?" Iliana started talking fast. "Maybe it is only stress."

"Stress?" The astonishment was evident in the tone of his voice.

"Yes, comrade. Filip, I mean Comrade Kozhevnikov said he was doing important work for the Party and the Service. Isn't that true?"

"Not anymore."

Kozhevnikov squeezed his eyes shut as tight as he could, desperately seeking to return to the dream, but it was no use. All he kept hearing were Grubkin's words *not anymore*. He opened his eyes and saw the pair of security thugs standing in front of him. It was then that he realized that he had never really been dreaming at all, that all this was the beginning of a nightmare to come.

✗   ✗   ✗   ✗

"**A**ssez piquant," The Quiet Man with the cover name of Cuthwick told the waiter. Spicy, that was the way he always enjoyed his steak tartare. And it was always good at this restaurant. Kozhevnikov had not turned up for the meet at the appointed time and place or at the fall back location. There was nothing more they could do. And why should they even try? The ZIL limousine from the Soviet Embassy no longer made its weekly trip to the French Party headquarters to deposit and later collect the First Secretary. Undoubtedly, their operation had been a success. "And I think the Bordeaux has had enough time to breathe."

He said nothing while the server picked up the decanter and poured some of the Lynch-Bages 1982 into his glass and waited for the Quiet Man to sip it before pouring more. He waved languidly at the man, indicating to just go ahead and finish pouring. After adding wine to his glass and that of the young man sitting across the table from him, he set the decanter down and left.

The young man picked up his glass and, holding it by the stem, swirled it expertly and sniffed at the rim. The Quiet Man did the same and then both of them sipped and let the liquid roll around on their palates and tongues before swallowing.

"Excellent," the Quiet Man said in his soft, quiet voice. "Long on the finish."

"Unlike our operation. Do you think Kozhevnikov is back in Moscow? They seemed to have gotten on to him rather quickly."

"What's the longevity of a turned agent? Especially one who has fulfilled his purpose." The Quiet Man regarded his glass of wine. "Saved us the trouble of grassing him, I suppose."

"What do you think he told them?"

"Everything. In the end, they always tell them everything, at least everything that they know. Even if they don't yet know they know it."

The young man whose operational name had been Geoffrey frowned. 'Will they try and double him back on us?"

The Quiet Man lifted a forkful of the raw filet mignon into his mouth, chewed and swallowed. "Moscow Center wouldn't waste the effort of doubling a staff slave like Kozhevnikov. If he's lucky, he'll be sent to a military battalion in Afghanistan; if not, then ...." He let that thought hang in the air while he sipped some of his wine.

"So Moscow Center believes that the Frenchy, Dubos, the Red that is the Party liaison with the Sandanistas in Nicaragua, is a double agent?"

The Quiet Man called Cuthwick took off his spectacles and polished them on the linen table napkin. "It is genetically impossible for them to think otherwise." He smiled and placed his spectacles back on his face. The KGB mindset always worked in our favor. He would just sit back and let their paranoia do all the work. They would inform the Sandinistas and even the Cuban DGS that Dubos was an imperialist spy.

"And what do you think will happen to him? Will Moscow inform the French Party?" His companion had a worried a look on his face. "Will he be hurt in all this?"

"I imagine not. At least not in the usual way. Perhaps on his next trip to Nicaragua there will be a fatal accident or illness."

"And that's the end of it?"

"Good heavens, no. It's just getting started; we'll leak to the French press that Dubos was murdered by the Sandinistas on orders from Moscow. Then we'll sit back and enjoy the fireworks."

"Won't the Russians retaliate against us?"

The Quiet Man laughed. "*Us*? Just who are *us*? Kozhevnikov was convinced that we are British. After all, what could be more indicative of the Brits than the proper use of the subjunctive in speech? I'll wager that somewhere between the extraction of the fourth and fifth molars without anesthesia, he has convinced his debriefers of the same. So if they go after anyone, it will be London. We've put a rather jolly good show, don't you think?"

"It would appear so. Certainly worth this bottle of wine."

The Quiet Man smiled again and held up his glass to the light. "Yes, it's big-boned with plenty of flesh. Quite the treat. Now let's finish this bottle and order another."

What the Quiet Man, smug with success, didn't realize was that he might have had an even better treat, also big-boned with plenty of flesh. For there had been Iliana, the gatekeeper to the *residentura's* strongroom and all its treasure. A woman smitten with a hapless dreamer and who would have done anything to be with him. Iliana, who had her own rude awakening and who, through no fault of her own, had joined her dear Filip in the dank subcellars of the Lubyanka where she was now telling her interrogators about all her dreams. ✗

Stan Trybulski, author of *One Trick Pony* and other crime novels, was a Brooklyn felony trial prosecutor before he went into private practice. Before he entered the legal profession, he was a newspaper reporter, college administrator and bartender (not all at the same time). He now divides his time between France and "two acres of Connecticut tranquility."

THE TAHITIAN POWDER BOX MYSTERY

by James Holding

CLASSIC REPRINT DEPARTMENT

INTRODUCTION

"The Tahitian Powder Box Mystery" was originally published in *Ellery Queen's Mystery Magazine*, October 1964. It is part of the "Leroy King" series by James Holding—which features writing partners Martin Leroy and King Danforth (who bear a striking similarity to the writing team of the "Ellery Queen" mysteries, Frederic Dannay and Manfred Lee)! Martin & King travel the world, vacationing with their wives, and solve mysteries along the way. The titles sound like Ellery Queen novels, too—"The Zanzibar Shirt Mystery," "The Norwegian Apple Mystery," etc.

EQMM's then-editor, none other than Frederic Dannay himself, must have enjoyed the Leroy King stories quite a bit...he published ten of them over the years, and even hired Holding to ghostwrite the "Ellery Queen, Jr." young adult mysteries. (James Holding, Samuel McCoy, and Frank Belknap Long wrote the whole 11-book E.Q., Jr. series between the three of them.)

The bare bones of Holding's life are well documented: born James Clark Carlisle Holding, Jr. on April 27, 1907, in Ben Avon, Pennsylvania. Parents: James Clark Carlisle (an engineer) and Laura May Holding (née Krepps). Died: age 89, from a stroke, on March 30, 1997.

Holding was, by all reports, a bright, ambitious, energetic youth. He attended Yale University, where he was a member of the Alpha Chi Rho fraternity, and graduated with an A.B. in 1928. After graduation, he spent a year exploring Europe. When he returned home, he took a sales job, but soon found a more creative calling in advertising as junior copywriter for the ad company Batte, Barton, Durstine & Osborne in Pittsburgh. In 1931, he married Janet Spice, with whom he had two children, James C.C. Holding III (1933-

2010) and Donald Angus Holding (1937-1953).

His career in advertizing proved successful. He rose swiftly in the ranks to copywriter, then in 1944 became copy chief. He created such advertising slogans as "Fort Pitt, That's It!" for Fort Pitt Beer. In 1952, he became vice-president of BBD&O.

Tragedy struck in 1953, with the death of his second son, Donald, in a beach accident while vacationing in Canada. The boy was only 16. James Holding took it hard, and it affected his advertising work. Ultimately he stepped down as Vice President from BBD&O (though he would remain as a consultant for the next decade). Instead, he focused his attention on a lifelong dream—a career as a writer. He set about it with the same drive and determination which made him a successful advertising executive, and the results of his labors were immediate: 1959 saw the sales of his first nine short stories, starting with "An Accident in Honiaria," which appeared in *Alfred Hitchcock's Mystery Magazine*, and "The Treasure of Pachacamac," which appeared in *Ellery Queen's Mystery Magazine* (both published in June 1960). He also cracked the lucrative children's picture-book market with *The Lazy Little Zulu* (beautifully illustrated by Aliki Brandenberg), his first hardcover, in 1962. More than 250 short stories and poems and 20 children's books would follow.

Mystery stories were his forté when writing for adults. He published prolifically in all the leading magazines of the day: *Alfred Hitchcock's Mystery Magazine, Ellery Queen's Mystery Magazine, Mike Shayne's Mystery Magazine, The Saint Mystery Magazine, The Man from U.N.C.L.E. Magazine*, and many others. Often he had stories in several simultaneously.

He created a number of long-running series over his 30-year career. "The Photographer" series features Manuel Andradas, a Brazilian hitman who disguises himself as a photographer. Andradas is a moral (relatively) killer, who doesn't always carry out his assignments to the letter. But you can believe the person he ultimately kills is the one who really deserved it.

Holding won the John Masefield Poetry Prize and the John Hubbard Curtis Poetry Prize twice. He and wife Janet "retired" (though writers never *really* retire!) to Sarasota, Florida, in 1971, but returned to Pennsylvania in 1991 when their health began to fail. The couple spent their last years at the Sherwood Oaks Retirement Home.

James Holding's last mystery story, "A Visitor to Monbasa," was published in *Alfred Hitchcock's Mystery Magazine* in June, 1992—exactly 32 years after his first professional appearance there. It is a fitting coda to a long and distinguished career in the mystery field.

In early 2015, Wildside Press purchased James Holding's copyrights from his daughter-in-law and has been working to reissue his work. A complete collection of the "Leroy King" series is forthcoming from Crippen & Landru in 2017.

—John Betancourt

✗ ✗ ✗ ✗

From a porthole on the *Valhalla's* sundeck a bare, slender, human arm suddenly appeared, thrust outward from the shoulder. The hand at the end of the arm tilted a round shallow box and dumped the contents casually into the purple swells that sucked at the ship's seaward side as she lay alongside the dock in Papeete.

Then the arm withdrew, having first paused briefly to tap the cardboard container against the ship's side and thus dislodge the final clinging grains of the box's contents.

Nobody saw this happen the first time.

But on the upper sundeck, directly above the porthole, the Danforths and Leroys stood at the ship's rail, raptly regarding the spectacular Tahitian sunset that was now painting the sky behind Moorea with gold and vermilion. And Helen Leroy, sniffing delicately, said, "You may not believe it, but this is absolutely the first perfumed sunset I ever saw. Or smelled, rather."

"Perfumed?" her husband asked absently, watching the changing colors of sky and sea.

"Yes, perfumed. Don't you smell it?"

"I do," Carol Danforth said, also sniffing. "And it's not any cheap, tawdry, domestic perfume, either. That's Chanel Number Five in my opinion. And my opinion is pretty expert!"

King Danforth said, "Are you out of your mind? Tahiti is reputedly romantic, I admit. But *perfumed* sunsets!"

"I smell it, too," Leroy said with surprise. "Take a deep breath, King. The girls are right."

Danforth followed instructions. "So l smell something nice," he conceded. "Flowers on the island perhaps? Frangipani? Jasmine?"

"That's Chanel Number Five," Carol insisted. And sneezed.

Martin Leroy sneezed, too. "Chanel, maybe," he said then, "but powder, not perfume. Look. That's what's making us sneeze."

He pointed to a mist of fine particles being lifted in a fragrant cloud over the rail by a gentle updraft of the sunset breeze.

Danforth said, "Somebody must be jettisoning bath powder out of her porthole somewhere below us."

"Who'd throw away Chanel powder, I'd like to know?" Helen said indignantly. "Let me look." She stretched up on her toes and leaned out over the rail. They all stared downward.

As they watched, an arm and hand emerged from the porthole below them and emptied the contents of a box into the sea. A light cloud of powder quickly dispersed on the air. When the arm withdrew, Leroy said, "That's one way to cut your inventory in a hurry."

"If you don't care about your overhead," quipped Danforth as Leroy sneezed once more.

"I think it's a vulgar gesture," Helen said. "Why not just quietly put the box of powder in her cabin wastebasket if she wants to get rid of it?" She turned to Carol. "I wonder who she is?"

Carol tossed her dark head. "I'll count the portholes from the back of the ship and find out," she said.

"Later," Danforth interposed. He glanced at his watch. "We've got to get moving. The dinner tour for Les Tropiques is supposed to gather on the dock right now."

"Then let's go," Leroy said with enthusiasm. "We don't want to miss the dancing girls!"

✗   ✗   ✗   ✗

The Tahitian dancing girls were very good. Even Helen and Carol admired their grace, sinuosity, and curiously Caucasian beauty. And the dinner at Les Tropiques restaurant was very good, too.

Their table was set in a corner of the wide terrace that faced the lagoon. As they ate, darkness gradually dimmed the outlines of the terrace and hid the faint line of white surf breaking over the reef, far out. Down the coast to their right, festive strings of colored lights marked the *Valhalla* at her pier. At full dark, native boys with torches in their hands came and lighted oil lamps around the edges of the terrace to illuminate the wild, hip-swaying movements of the Tahitian dance troupe.

Danforth breathed a sigh of purest satisfaction and said, "I never thought I'd live to see the day that a travel folder understated the case for a tourist attraction."

"I take it you like Tahiti," Helen said, laughing. She looked at the dancers in their grass skirts and straw bras, their bare golden flesh burnished by the leaping flare of the oil lamps, and she smiled at Carol.

"Like it?" said Danforth. "It gets me right here." He tapped his chest.

John Rich, a fellow passenger from the *Valhalla*, was sitting at the next table with three loquacious widows. He leaned over and said with a grin, "I heard that, Mr. Danforth. And how right you are! Isn't this great?" Rich was a bachelor, slim, dark-eyed, fortyish, with formal good manners but a slightly raffish air. He was very popular with the *Valhalla* passengers, especially the unattached women. It was rumored he had been the chauffeur-houseman of a recently deceased Detroit industrialist who had remembered him generously in his will. This cruise, the ship's gossip ran, was in the nature of a celebration of his newfound independence.

Leroy replied, "It's great, all right. We can't afford to go too far overboard, though—not with our wives sitting here with us!"

Rich laughed and indicated his table companions. "I haven't got a wife," he said, "but my harem, here, is trying to make me put on the brakes. I've already warned them that I'm striking out on my own right after dinner!"

"Good hunting," Leroy said.

The dinner party broke up just then in a burst of applause for the native dancers.

✗   ✗   ✗   ✗

Quinn's, the most famous saloon in the South Seas, was a madhouse when they arrived some time later. Almost every able-bodied passenger from the *Valhalla* was there, it seemed, and a raucous mob of French, Polynesians, Melanesians, Orientals, and mixtures thereof swelled the uproar. Everybody in the place appeared to be either laughing shrilly, shouting for drinks, beating beer glasses on the scarred table tops, singing drunkenly, or publicly romancing the unashamed native B-girls.

The Danforths and Leroys found a table as far from the bar as possible and ordered stingers.

They were no sooner seated than Carol said, "There's John Rich over there."

They looked across the wide room and saw John Rich standing at the end of the bar. He was talking to a barefooted Polynesian girl clad in a low-cut island dress of figured red cotton. The girl's long straight hair poured down her back like a black waterfall.

"He's found himself a Polynesian houri, I see," Leroy said dreamily. "And not bad, either!"

Danforth said, "You know what? That girl with Rich is one of the girls who were selling flowers on the porch of Les Tropiques when we came out."

"You must have studied her with considerable care to be able to recognize her across a mad place like this at forty paces," Helen teased him. "For the life of me, I can't see what's so terribly attractive to you men about bare feet and long straight black hair." Helen was an ethereally lovely blonde.

"Bare feet!" Leroy laughed. "Are her feet bare, too?"

Danforth said, "She reminds me of something."

"Of what?" This was from Carol. "Whistler's mother?"

With studied restraint Danforth answered, "No, but something rather curious. After dinner I waited on the porch of Les Tropiques while you three visited the washrooms, remember? John Rich came out of the restaurant while I was waiting. He stopped on the porch and said something to that girl he's with over there. She was selling flowers then."

"Asking her for a date," said Helen. "He said he was going a-wolfing. What's strange about that?"

"He was speaking Italian," Danforth said softly.

"Italian?" Leroy raised his eyebrows. "You sure?"

"Or Latin."

"John Rich speaking Latin?" Carol hooted.

"Maybe his real name is Ricci," Leroy hazarded, "in which case he might know Italian."

"True," said Danforth. "But what about the girl? Would *she* know Italian?"

"What makes you think she did?"

"She understood him—at least, she answered him without a moment's pause. In English. But the last word of Rich's question to her—that's all I heard—was definitely not in English. It was either Italian or Latin."

"What was the last word?"

"*Acuminata.* That's what he said. With a rising inflection, hence a question."

Leroy slapped the table and laughed. "I've always told you, King, if you want to be a well-rounded mystery novelist you should learn a little about everything—including botany. Only a modicum, mind you, but *something* about the flowers and fruits and—er—flora of our teeming planet."

"What are you drinking, Mart?" Helen asked sweetly. "Ambrosia? The birds and the bees will be next, no doubt."

"And I can't think of a better place than Tahiti for *that* lecture!" Carol added.

"Quiet, children," said Danforth, "your elders are speaking. Why flora, Mart?"

"And why not Cora, Dora, and Nora, if it comes to that?" Carol laughed.

"Because," Leroy pointed out patiently, "if you knew anything about the flora of these islands, King, you'd recognize that the Italian word you overheard John Rich using was merely a descriptive adjective, part of the botanical name for a genus of the frangipani plant."

"You're kidding," Danforth said.

"Not at all. I believe the full term is *plumeria acuminata*—meaning the sharp or pointed frangipani. White. As distinguished, let us say, from *plumeria rubra,* which is simply red jasmine flowers to us learned botanists." Leroy preened himself.

His wife exclaimed in astonishment, "Why, Mart, you never told me you knew so much about flowers! Will you address our garden club when you get home?"

"Gladly." Leroy bowed. "You can sign me up now by buying me another drink."

"Wait a minute," Danforth protested. He rubbed a hand over his crew-cut. "So Rich wasn't speaking Italian. But I still think it was odd for Rich to ask about the pointed frangipani, or whatever you called it, by its scientific name, don't you?"

Leroy nodded seriously. "You wouldn't think the average re-tired-type chauffeur from Detroit would know there was such a thing as frangipani, let alone what its correct botanical designation is."

Helen, who had been watching Rich across the saloon, spoke up. "New song title: 'He asked for *plumeria acuminata*, but he got red jasmine instead.' That lei around his neck is woven of pink flowers."

"If you would only let me finish," Danforth said, "I can explain that, too. In answer to Rich's question about *acuminata*, that girl over there stood up from among the flower sellers on the restaurant porch and said to Rich, 'Good evening, Monsieur, wouldn't you like this better?' And she hung that red jasmine lei around his neck, and they went off together, arm in arm."

"Just like that?" Helen asked.

"Just like that. So *she* picked *him* up, if you want my opinion, not the other way around."

"The hussy!" said Carol, waving across the room to John Rich and his companion. "How fascinating! Maybe they will join us."

She invited them to do so in vigorous sign language. Rich said something to the native girl in the red dress. She shook her head and turned back to the bar. Rich spread his hands in apology to Carol, then put his arm around the girl's bare shoulders. She turned a cool, remote smile on him then. But she seemed to be looking beyond him toward the door.

✗ ✗ ✗ ✗

For the next two days King Danforth and Martin Leroy, known to millions of mystery story fans as the author, "Leroy King," were so completely occupied with sightseeing and shopping in Tahiti that neither they nor their wives gave another thought to *plumeria acuminata* or Chanel Number Five bath powder.

It wasn't until the *Valhalla* was steaming out of Papeete harbor bound for Suva in the Fijis, that Carol Danforth, sipping her pre-prandial gimlet, said, "And now that we're back to normal ship-board scandal, I'm still curious to know who was throwing away Chanel bath powder the other day."

"I'm astonished at your ladylike patience," Leroy commented.

"I thought you'd have found out who she was long since."

Danforth lit a cigarette. "One thing is fairly obvious," he said idly, but with a challenging glance at his partner. "She isn't just an amateur powder-dumper, this gal. She's a professional."

"How do you reach that obscure conclusion?" Leroy asked.

"It leaps to the eye. The lady didn't throw away just one boxful of powder. She threw away at least two. That makes her a pro, doesn't it?"

Carol said, "What do you mean, she threw away two boxes of powder?"

"Remember you smelled the powder while we were watching the sunset? And saw some of it blowing over the rail? And sneezed because of it?"

"Yes."

"Well, that means she had already dumped one box of powder before the one we *saw* her dump. Because we didn't look down till afterward."

"Elementary," Leroy murmured. His expressive face lit up with the pleasure he always felt when engaging in this kind of deductive play with his partner. "But something else about the incident seemed of even more significance to me, if I may say so."

Danforth grinned. "Please say so."

"Cut it out, you two," Carol said plaintively. "You can't make a mystery out of this, not even in fun. I forbid it. We're on vacation. All I want to know is who the silly woman is who throws away Chanel Number Five powder."

"Please," Leroy said with an air of injured dignity, "doesn't anyone want to know what I deduced?"

"Of course, darling." Helen patted his hand. "Because I'm going to hear it anyway. But please make it short."

"Very well. I deduced that whoever was throwing away the powder wanted the empty box for another purpose. She didn't throw the whole package into the sea—just the powder."

"A sobering thought," Danforth acknowledged. "What could she want with two empty powder boxes?"

Helen laughed. "Maybe she wanted something to keep her old buttons and pins in. Or her false teeth at night."

"A distinct possibility," her husband said approvingly.

Abruptly, Carol said, "Pardon me a moment."

She went over and spoke to the bartender who smiled and handed her something from under the bar. She came back with what proved to be a deck plan of the *Valhalla*, showing all staterooms, portholes, showers, closets, bars, and other features of the ship.

"Now, then," Carol went on in a businesslike tone, "the porthole from which the powder-dumper was operating was the eighth from the stern." She carefully counted eight portholes from the rear of the ship's sundeck. "She lives in cabin S-34," Carol announced triumphantly.

"I'll run down to the Purser's Office and look at the list of cabins," Helen offered eagerly. "Then we'll know who she is."

Within five minutes Helen returned, obviously bursting with news. "It isn't a woman at all!"" she said. "How do you like that?"

"You mean there's no woman listed in Stateroom S-34?"

"Not one. It's a single cabin occupied exclusively by..." She paused dramatically. "By our bachelor friend, Mr. John Rich."

Leroy slowly put his drink down and straightened in his chair. His eyes met Danforth's. "A visiting lady, then?" he asked. "One of those widows he calls his 'harem'? Could that be the one who was dumping bath powder from his porthole?"

Danforth shook his head, frowning. "Not likely. But John Rich is small-boned, slender, and he has small hands. That bare arm from the porthole could have been *his*."

Leroy rubbed his jaw. "Well, well, well," he said softly, almost to himself. "If that's true, we have *two* incidents in which Mr. John Rich acted quite out of character—dumping powder into the ocean from his stateroom porthole, and using familiarly the scientific name of a tropical flower he shouldn't even know exists."

"Lots of people have flowers for a hobby, possibly ex-chauffeurs..." Helen began, but both men ignored her. They were suddenly as hot on the scent of this little mystery as though it were one of their own fictional plots.

"Suppose," said Leroy, "it *was* John Rich dumping bath powder, where would he have got it?"

"Right here on the ship," Carol said. "The shop sells French perfume, soap, and powder at very low prices."

"Say he bought the powder on the ship, then. Why?"

"Not for gifts to take home," Danforth said, "because he threw the stuff away. Therefore, he must have wanted empty powder boxes."

"Exactly. Again, why?"

"To hold something else, as you brilliantly deduced."

"But why buy expensive Chanel and waste it, just to get empty boxes? Why not the cheapest possible brand?"

"Ah," said Danforth, smiling, "one can but guess as to that. My guess is that Rich wants somebody—perhaps the customs officials in New York at the end of this cruise—to *think* he's bringing home a few gift boxes of Chanel powder, when he's really bringing home something else."

"Now that," Leroy grinned, "is a truly brilliant hypothesis to which I subscribe whole-heartedly. Respectable Chanel powder containers would be smuggling camouflage of the highest order for whatever John Rich fills them with."

Helen said in a resigned tone, "The next question before the house, therefore, is this: What does John Rich intend to fill the powder boxes with?"

"I withdraw my suggestion about buttons and pins," Helen volunteered.

"Thank you." Danforth swung one leg over the arm of his chair. "Since he was emptying the boxes at Papeete, one might reasonably assume that he meant to fill them with something he intended to get in Tahiti."

"Any ideas?" Leroy asked.

"Dancing girls," said Carol. "Think how the boys would go for Tahitian bunnies in our key clubs at home!"

"Be serious, child," Leroy rebuked her. "Great minds are at work here. And your frivolity impedes smooth cerebration. Well, King?"

Danforth shrugged. "Whatever it was, I'll wager the flower girl who picked him up at Les Tropiques had something to do with it."

Leroy started visibly. He said with a trace of excitement, "That's it, by Jove!"

"What's it?" Helen demanded.

"I'll bet John Rich was using a prearranged recognition signal when he went through that *plumeria acuminata* bit—to identify himself to the flower girl."

"Of course!" Danforth tapped his fingers nervously on the table. "And the flower girl gives him a prearranged response and the red jasmine lei as the other half of the signal. That's why they became old buddies immediately and were in Quinn's together. They had some kind of deal cooking."

"Sex appeal alone drew them together, if you want to know what I think," Carol said. "I could tell by the way Rich looked at her!"

"But not," Leroy said thoughtfully, "by the way she looked at him. She kept brushing off Rich's passes at the bar and watching Quinn's door as though she were expecting someone."

"Her principal, you mean?" said Danforth. "The boss smuggler, maybe? You think she was assigned to pick Rich out of our tourist group and take him to her leader at Quinn's?"

"Something like that makes sense." Leroy absent-mindedly reached over and finished his wife's gimlet.

"Now that you've had your cocktail, darling," his wife said with deceptive sweetness, "it's well past dinner time. Come on. Forget John Rich, please. There's roast reindeer tonight."

Danforth and Leroy docilely followed their wives to the dining room.

✗   ✗   ✗   ✗

With the last bite of dessert, however—something their Norwegian table steward referred to as "peaches pie"—the two mystery writers returned to their speculations.

"Tahiti," Leroy ruminated aloud, "produces nothing much but breadfruit, mangoes, taro root, copra, girls, climate, and leisure, not necessarily in that order. And none of these would fit comfortably into a Chanel powder box."

"It occurred to me during the reindeer steak," said Danforth, "that Tahiti may be merely a way station, a pickup point, for whatever it is that Rich is smuggling."

"It's isolated enough, all right. In the middle of the Pacific, halfway between Asia and everywhere else. Let's see. Asia. From Asia, one smuggles embroideries and jade originating in Red China, oriental workmen who will work elsewhere for peanuts—"

Danforth snapped his fingers. "Why not the obvious answer?"

Politely Leroy inquired, "And what is the obvious answer, Professor? As if we didn't know."

"Think of boxes full of white powder. Think of Red China.

Think of—"

"Heroin?"

"What else?"

"From the beginning," Leroy murmured, "it seemed clearly indicated."

Carol lifted her eyes to the ceiling and said, "You poor, mystery-happy idiots!"

Danforth ignored her. "There's more than a chance, Mart," he said, "that John Rich is not a retired chauffeur, but a member of some dope-peddling organization in the United States. He takes this round-the-world cruise solely for the purpose of picking up a shipment of heroin in Tahiti, where—by equally devious means—it has arrived from Hong Kong or Red China. Rich is seemingly above suspicion—an innocent tourist on a cruise."

Leroy took it up. "Right. Rich identifies himself to his Tahitian colleagues as the courier sent from America to pick up the heroin, by an exchange of prearranged code phrases with the flower girl, of which *plumeria acuminata* is undoubtedly one. After he has identified himself, the heroin is passed to him—perhaps in Quinn's—where the confusion would cover up *any* monkey business. Rich then conceals the heroin in the Chanel powder boxes he has prepared in his cabin.

"At the end of the cruise he calmly carries the heroin through customs, having dutifully entered several gift boxes of Chanel Number Five powder on his customs declaration, all according to regulations. The heroin powder in genuine Chanel boxes would almost certainly go undetected, even by a careful inspection which, incidentally, returning cruise passengers arc seldom subjected to. Is that it?"

"That's exactly it," Danforth said. "So let's go ask the Captain to have Rich's cabin searched for the heroin. If it's there, the Captain can tip the Narcotics and Customs Bureaus by radio-telephone and have them catch Rich red-handed as he comes ashore in New York."

Leroy turned to Carol and Helen. "Will you excuse us?" he asked. "We'll meet you in the toward lounge later." He and Danforth stood up.

Helen said, "Are you really going to Captain Hansen with that crazy story?"

"Certainly," her husband answered. "As conscientious American citizens..."

"But it's completely fantastic!" Carol broke in. "From an empty powder box and the name of a tropical flower, you deduce an international dope ring operating on this ship! Now really!"

"We didn't *make* a mystery out of this thing," Leroy defended himself. "We've merely made logical deductions from observed facts, that's all."

Carol and Helen looked at each other and suddenly dissolved in laughter.

"What's so funny?" Leroy asked.

"You!" his wife managed to gasp through her laughter. "You and your 'observed facts'! That's what's funny!" She and Helen struggled to contain their mirth. "But you're perfectly right when you say that you and King didn't make a mystery out of this."

"He did," Helen crowed.

Slowly Danforth and Leroy resumed their seats. They watched their wives like wary baby-sitters observing unfamiliar and obstreperous charges.

"Don't be cross with us, darlings," Carol said, "but one of the facts on which you based your deductions was slightly wrong. And it's our fault."

"What fact?" Leroy King spoke sharply.

"The number of the cabin from which the arm dumped the powder out the porthole."

"It wasn't S-34?"

"No. It was S-36."

"You said it was the eighth porthole from the stern," Leroy reminded her.

"I know. But it really wasn't. I fibbed. It was the ninth."

Danforth said to Helen, "And *you* looked it up and told us it was occupied, that cabin, by John Rich!" He looked at her accusingly. "What for?"

"Just for laughs," Helen chortled. "To see what you master-plotters would make of it. And you haven't disappointed us one bit, have they, Carol?"

Danforth summoned a rueful grin. "These women we call our wives," he said to his partner, "call powerfully to mind a single old-fashioned word: perfidious."

Leroy nodded. "At the very least," he agreed. Then he asked his wife curiously, "Who *does* occupy cabin S-36 if John Rich doesn't?"

"Two of the widows in John Rich's 'harem' occupy it—the cabin is a double."

"And it was one of them who threw away the powder?"

"They had each," Carol explained, "bought a box of Chanel Number Five powder for use on this trip from the shop. But Mrs. Piggott, the older of the two, proved allergic to Chanel powder. It made her sneeze dreadfully. So she threw the powder out the porthole."

"And her roommate?"

"She very obligingly threw hers out, too, since she couldn't use it without causing Mrs. Piggott distress. And she'd already opened her box."

"But why save the boxes?"

Carol laughed. "Mrs. Piggott is going to the masquerade ball tomorrow night as a typical cruise shopper, with bargain items she's bought on this trip draped all over her. She decided the two empty powder boxes would make a good addition to her masquerade costume. So she saved them to wear."

"Well, well," Leroy murmured. His lean face, surprisingly, reflected pride and affection rather than anger as he contemplated his wife's duplicity. "When did you find all this out?" he asked curiously.

"In the ladies' washroom at Les Tropiques after dinner that night," Helen said. "You know how girls talk in places like that! And there was some powder there that made Mrs. Piggott sneeze, which got her started on the subject."

"And I suppose," said Danforth with an injured air, "you also knew all about Rich's use of *plumeria acuminata* to the flower girl on the porch?"

Helen said, "Mrs. Piggott used to be a botany teacher, didn't you know? As a member of John Rich's 'harem,' I'm sure she had talked to him on some of the local Tahitian blooms. And I guess John Rich just used the *plumeria* name to show off to the half-naked flower girl—you know, impress her with the fact that he knew something about Tahiti."

Carol said, "I *told* you it was sex appeal alone that drew them together."

"Very likely." Leroy called the wine steward and ordered a B & B for each of them. When it came, he looked over his tiny glass at his partner and remarked with a grin. "Well, King, even if we were wrong about it, I wouldn't say we completely wasted our time on this powder box mystery, would you?"

"By no means," Danforth replied sardonically. "Far from it. Just think, I shall never again be ignorant of the proper name tor a pointed white frangipani flower! This is not to be lightly regarded."

"I didn't mean that," Leroy said. "I meant that we've been forcibly brought face to face in this business with the greatest enigma of them all—with the only mystery that even Leroy King may never be able to solve."

Helen and Carol dropped their eyes modestly. Carol kicked Helen under the table. "I think they mean *us*," she said wickedly. "Aren't they cute?"

✗

THE ADVENTURE OF THE CARDBOARD BOX

by Sir Arthur Conan Doyle

In choosing a few typical cases which illustrate the remarkable mental qualities of my friend, Sherlock Holmes, I have endeavoured, as far as possible, to select those which presented the minimum of sensationalism, while offering a fair field for his talents. It is, however, unfortunately impossible entirely to separate the sensational from the criminal, and a chronicler is left in the dilemma that he must either sacrifice details which are essential to his statement and so give a false impression of the problem, or he must use matter which chance, and not choice, has provided him with. With this short preface I shall turn to my notes of what proved to be a strange, though a peculiarly terrible, chain of events.

It was a blazing hot day in August. Baker Street was like an oven, and the glare of the sunlight upon the yellow brickwork of the house across the road was painful to the eye. It was hard to believe that these were the same walls which loomed so gloomily through the fogs of winter. Our blinds were half-drawn, and Holmes lay curled upon the sofa, reading and re-reading a letter which he had received by the morning post. For myself, my term of service in India had trained me to stand heat better than cold, and a thermometer at ninety was no hardship. But the morning paper was uninteresting. Parliament had risen. Everybody was out of town, and I yearned for the glades of the New Forest or the shingle of Southsea. A depleted bank account had caused me to postpone my holiday, and as to my companion, neither the country nor the sea presented the slightest attraction to him. He loved to lie in the very center of five millions of people, with his filaments stretching out and running through them, responsive to every little rumour or suspicion of unsolved crime. Appreciation of nature found no place among his many gifts, and his only change was when he turned his mind from the evil-doer of the town to track down his brother of the country.

Finding that Holmes was too absorbed for conversation I had tossed aside the barren paper, and leaning back in my chair I fell into a brown study. Suddenly my companion's voice broke in upon my thoughts:

"You are right, Watson," said he. "It does seem a most preposterous way of settling a dispute."

"Most preposterous!" I exclaimed, and then suddenly realizing how he had echoed the inmost thought of my soul, I sat up in my chair and stared at him in blank amazement. "What is this, Holmes?" I cried. "This is beyond anything which I could have imagined."

He laughed heartily at my perplexity.

"You remember," said he, "that some little time ago when I read you the passage in one of Poe's sketches in which a close reasoner follows the unspoken thoughts of his companion, you were inclined to treat the matter as a mere *tour-de-force* of the author. On my remarking that I was constantly in the habit of doing the same thing you expressed incredulity."

"Oh, no!"

"Perhaps not with your tongue, my dear Watson, but certainly with your eyebrows. So when I saw you throw down your paper and enter upon a train of thought, I was very happy to have the opportunity of reading it off, and eventually of breaking into it, as a proof that I had been in rapport with you."

But I was still far from satisfied. "In the example which you read to me," said I, "the reasoner drew his conclusions from the actions of the man whom he observed. If I remember right, he stumbled over a heap of stones, looked up at the stars, and so on. But I have been seated quietly in my chair, and what clues can I have given you?"

"You do yourself an injustice. The features are given to man as the means by which he shall express his emotions, and yours are faithful servants."

"Do you mean to say that you read my train of thoughts from my features?"

"Your features and especially your eyes. Perhaps you cannot yourself recall how your reverie commenced?"

"No, I cannot."

"Then I will tell you. After throwing down your paper, which was the action which drew my attention to you, you sat for half a minute with a vacant expression. Then your eyes fixed themselves upon your newly framed picture of General Gordon, and I saw by the alteration in your face that a train of thought had been started. But it did not lead very far. Your eyes flashed across to the un-framed portrait of Henry Ward Beecher which stands upon the top of your books. Then you glanced up at the wall, and of course your meaning was obvious. You were thinking that if the portrait were framed it would just cover that bare space and correspond with Gordon's picture there."

"You have followed me wonderfully!" I exclaimed.

"So far I could hardly have gone astray. But now your thoughts went back to Beecher, and you looked hard across as if you were studying the character in his features. Then your eyes ceased to pucker, but you continued to look across, and your face was thoughtful. You were recalling the incidents of Beecher's career. I was well aware that you could not do this without thinking of the mission which he undertook on behalf of the North at the time of the Civil War, for I remember your expressing your passion-ate indignation at the way in which he was received by the more turbulent of our people. You felt so strongly about it that I knew you could not think of Beecher without thinking of that also. When a moment later I saw your eyes wander away from the picture, I suspected that your mind had now turned to the Civil War, and when I observed that your lips set, your eyes sparkled, and your hands clenched I was positive that you were indeed thinking of the gallantry which was shown by both sides in that desperate struggle. But then, again, your face grew sadder, you shook your head. You were dwelling upon the sadness and horror and useless waste of life. Your hand stole towards your own old wound and a smile quivered on your lips, which showed me that the ridiculous side of this method of settling international questions had forced itself upon your mind. At this point I agreed with you that it was preposterous and was glad to find that all my deductions had been correct."

"Absolutely!" said I. "And now that you have explained it, I confess that I am as amazed as before."

"It was very superficial, my dear Watson, I assure you. I should not have intruded it upon your attention had you not shown some incredulity the other day. But I have in my hands here a little problem which may prove to be more difficult of solution than my small essay in thought reading. Have you observed in the paper a short paragraph referring to the remarkable contents of a packet sent through the post to Miss Cushing, of Cross Street, Croydon?"

"No, I saw nothing."

"Ah! then you must have overlooked it. Just toss it over to me. Here it is, under the financial column. Perhaps you would be good enough to read it aloud."

I picked up the paper which he had thrown back to me and read the paragraph indicated. It was headed, "A Gruesome Packet."

> Miss Susan Cushing, living at Cross Street, Croydon, has been made the victim of what must be regarded as a peculiarly revolting practical joke unless some more sinister meaning should prove to be attached to the incident. At two o'clock yesterday afternoon a small packet, wrapped in brown paper, was handed in by the postman. A cardboard box was inside, which was filled with coarse salt. On emptying this, Miss Cushing was horrified to find two human ears, apparently quite freshly severed. The box had been sent by parcel post from Belfast upon the morning before. There is no indication as to the sender, and the matter is the more mysterious as Miss Cushing, who is a maiden lady of fifty, has led a most retired life, and has so few acquaintances or correspondents that it is a rare event for her to receive anything through the post. Some years ago, however, when she resided at Penge, she let apartments in her house to three young medical students, whom she was obliged to get rid of on account of their noisy and irregular habits. The police are of opinion that this outrage may have been perpetrated upon Miss Cushing by these youths, who owed her a grudge and who hoped to frighten her by sending her these relics of the dissecting-rooms. Some probability is lent to the theory by the fact that one of these students came from the north of Ireland, and, to the best of Miss Cushing's belief, from Belfast. In the meantime, the matter is being actively investigated, Mr Lestrade, one of the very smartest of our detective officers, being in charge of the case.

"So much for the *Daily Chronicle*," said Holmes as I finished reading. "Now for our friend Lestrade. I had a note from him this morning, in which he says:

"'I think that this case is very much in your line. We have every hope of clearing the matter up, but we find a little difficulty in getting anything to work upon. We have, of course, wired to the Belfast post-office, but a large number of parcels were handed in upon that day, and they have no means of identifying this particular one, or of remembering the sender. The box is a half-pound box of honeydew tobacco and does not help us in any way. The medical student theory still appears to me to be the most feasible, but if you should have a few hours to spare I should be very happy to see you out here. I shall be either at the house or in the police-station all day.'

"What say you, Watson? Can you rise superior to the heat and run down to Croydon with me on the off chance of a case for your annals?"

"I was longing for something to do."

"You shall have it, then. Ring for our boots and tell them to order a cab. I'll be back in a moment when I have changed my dressing-gown and filled my cigar-case."

A shower of rain fell while we were in the train, and the heat was far less oppressive in Croydon than in town. Holmes had sent on a wire, so that Lestrade, as wiry, as dapper, and as ferret-like as ever, was waiting for us at the station. A walk of five minutes took us to Cross Street, where Miss Cushing resided.

It was a very long street of two-story brick houses, neat and prim, with whitened stone steps and little groups of aproned women gossiping at the doors. Halfway down, Lestrade stopped and tapped at a door, which was opened by a small servant girl. Miss Cushing was sitting in the front room, into which we were ushered. She was a placid-faced woman, with large, gentle eyes, and grizzled hair curving down over her temples on each side. A worked antimacassar lay upon her lap and a basket of coloured silks stood upon a stool beside her.

"They are in the outhouse, those dreadful things," said she as Lestrade entered. "I wish that you would take them away altogether."

"So I shall, Miss Cushing. I only kept them here until my friend, Mr Holmes, should have seen them in your presence."

"Why in my presence, sir?"

"In case he wished to ask any questions."

"What is the use of asking me questions when I tell you I know nothing whatever about it?"

"Quite so, madam," said Holmes in his soothing way. "I have no doubt that you have been annoyed more than enough already over this business."

"Indeed I have, sir. I am a quiet woman and live a retired life. It is something new for me to see my name in the papers and to find the police in my house. I won't have those things in here, Mr Lestrade. If you wish to see them you must go to the outhouse."

It was a small shed in the narrow garden which ran behind the house. Lestrade went in and brought out a yellow cardboard box, with a piece of brown paper and some string. There was a bench at the end of the path, and we all sat down while Homes examined one by one, the articles which Lestrade had handed to him.

"The string is exceedingly interesting," he remarked, holding it up to the light and sniffing at it. "What do you make of this string, Lestrade?"

"It has been tarred."

"Precisely. It is a piece of tarred twine. You have also, no doubt, remarked that Miss Cushing has cut the cord with a scissors, as can be seen by the double fray on each side. This is of importance."

"I cannot see the importance," said Lestrade.

"The importance lies in the fact that the knot is left intact, and that this knot is of a peculiar character."

"It is very neatly tied. I had already made a note to that effect," said Lestrade complacently.

"So much for the string, then," said Holmes, smiling, "now for the box wrapper. Brown paper, with a distinct smell of coffee. What, did you not observe it? I think there can be no doubt of it. Address printed in rather straggling characters: 'Miss S. Cushing, Cross Street, Croydon.' Done with a broad-pointed pen, probably a J, and with very inferior ink. The word 'Croydon' has been originally spelled with an 'i', which has been changed to 'y'. The parcel was directed, then, by a man—the printing is distinctly masculine—of limited education and unacquainted with the town of Croydon. So far, so good! The box is a yellow, half-pound honeydew box, with nothing distinctive save two thumb marks at the left bottom corner. It is filled with rough salt of the quality used for preserving hides and other of the coarser commercial purposes. And embedded in it are these very singular enclosures."

He took out the two ears as he spoke, and laying a board across his knee he examined them minutely, while Lestrade and I, bending forward on each side of him, glanced alternately at these dreadful relics and at the thoughtful, eager face of our companion. Finally he returned them to the box once more and sat for a while in deep meditation.

"You have observed, of course," said he at last, "that the ears are not a pair."

"Yes, I have noticed that. But if this were the practical joke of some students from the dissecting-rooms, it would be as easy for them to send two odd ears as a pair."

"Precisely. But this is not a practical joke."

"You are sure of it?"

"The presumption is strongly against it. Bodies in the dissect-ing-rooms are injected with preservative fluid. These ears bear no signs of this. They are fresh, too. They have been cut off with a blunt instrument, which would hardly happen if a student had done it. Again, carbolic or rectified spirits would be the preservatives which would suggest themselves to the medical mind, certainly not rough salt. I repeat that there is no practical joke here, but that we are investigating a serious crime."

A vague thrill ran through me as I listened to my companion's words and saw the stern gravity which had hardened his features. This brutal preliminary seemed to shadow forth some strange and inexplicable horror in the background. Lestrade, however, shook his head like a man who is only half convinced.

"There are objections to the joke theory, no doubt," said he, "but there are much stronger reasons against the other. We know that this woman has led a most quiet and respectable life at Penge and here for the last twenty years. She has hardly been away from her home for a day during that time. Why on earth, then, should any criminal send her the proofs of his guilt, especially as, unless she is a most consummate actress, she understands quite as little of the matter as we do?"

"That is the problem which we have to solve," Holmes answered, "and for my part I shall set about it by presuming that my reasoning is correct, and that a double murder has been committed. One of these ears is a woman's, small, finely formed, and pierced for an earring. The other is a man's, sun-burned, discoloured, and also pierced for an earring. These two people are presumably dead, or we should have heard their story before now. To-day is Friday. The packet was posted on Thursday morning. The tragedy, then, occurred on Wednesday or Tuesday, or earlier. If the two people were murdered, who but their murderer would have sent this sign of his work to Miss Cushing? We may take it that the sender of the packet is the man whom we want. But he must have some strong reason for sending Miss Cushing this packet. What reason then? It must have been to tell her that the deed was done; or to pain her, perhaps. But in that case she knows who it is. Does she know? I doubt it. If she knew, why should she call the police in? She might have buried the ears, and no one would have been the wiser. That is what she would have done if she had wished to shield the criminal. But if she does not wish to shield him she would give his name. There is a tangle here which needs straightening out." He had been talking in a high, quick voice, staring blankly up over the garden fence, but now he sprang briskly to his feet and walked towards the house.

"I have a few questions to ask Miss Cushing," said he.

"In that case I may leave you here," said Lestrade, "for I have another small business on hand. I think that I have nothing further to learn from Miss Cushing. You will find me at the police-station."

"We shall look in on our way to the train," answered Holmes. A moment later he and I were back in the front room, where the impassive lady was still quietly working away at her antimacassar. She put it down on her lap as we entered and looked at us with her frank, searching blue eyes.

"I am convinced, sir," she said, "that this matter is a mistake, and that the parcel was never meant for me at all. I have said this several times to the gentlemen from Scotland Yard, but he simply laughs at me. I have not an enemy in the world, as far as I know, so why should anyone play me such a trick?"

"I am coming to be of the same opinion, Miss Cushing," said Holmes, taking a seat beside her. "I think that it is more than probable—" He paused, and I was surprised, on glancing round to see that he was staring with singular intentness at the lady's profile. Surprise and satisfaction were both for an instant to be read upon his eager face, though when she glanced round to find out the cause of his silence he had become as demure as ever. I stared hard myself at her flat, grizzled hair, her trim cap, her little gilt earrings, her placid features; but I could see nothing which could account for my companion's evident excitement.

"There were one or two questions—"

"Oh, I am weary of questions!" cried Miss Cushing impatiently.

"You have two sisters, I believe."

"How could you know that?"

"I observed the very instant that I entered the room that you have a portrait group of three ladies upon the mantelpiece, one of whom is undoubtedly yourself, while the others are so exceedingly like you that there could be no doubt of the relationship."

"Yes, you are quite right. Those are my sisters, Sarah and Mary."

"And here at my elbow is another portrait, taken at Liverpool, of your younger sister, in the company of a man who appears to be a steward by his uniform. I observe that she was unmarried at the time."

"You are very quick at observing."

"That is my trade."

"Well, you are quite right. But she was married to Mr Browner a few days afterwards. He was on the South American line when that was taken, but he was so fond of her that he couldn't abide to leave her for so long, and he got into the Liverpool and London boats."

"Ah, the *Conqueror*, perhaps?"

"No, the *May Day*, when last I heard. Jim came down here to see me once. That was before he broke the pledge; but afterwards he would always take drink when he was ashore, and a little drink would send him stark, staring mad. Ah! it was a bad day that ever he took a glass in his hand again. First he dropped me, then he quarrelled with Sarah, and now that Mary has stopped writing we don't know how things are going with them."

It was evident that Miss Cushing had come upon a subject on which she felt very deeply. Like most people who lead a lonely life, she was shy at first, but ended by becoming extremely communicative. She told us many details about her brother-in-law the steward, and then wandering off on the subject of her former lodgers, the medical students, she gave us a long account of their delinquencies, with their names and those of their hospitals. Holmes listened attentively to everything, throwing in a question from time to time.

"About your second sister, Sarah," said he. "I wonder, since you are both maiden ladies, that you do not keep house together."

"Ah! you don't know Sarah's temper or you would wonder no more. I tried it when I came to Croydon, and we kept on until about two months ago, when we had to part. I don't want to say a word against my own sister, but she was always meddlesome and hard to please, was Sarah."

"You say that she quarrelled with your Liverpool relations."

"Yes, and they were the best of friends at one time. Why, she went up there to live in order to be near them. And now she has no word hard enough for Jim Browner. The last six months that she was here she would speak of nothing but his drinking and his ways. He had caught her meddling, I suspect, and given her a bit of his mind, and that was the start of it."

"Thank you, Miss Cushing," said Holmes, rising and bowing. "Your sister Sarah lives, I think you said, at New Street, Wallington? Good-bye, and I am very sorry that you should have been troubled over a case with which, as you say, you have nothing whatever to do."

There was a cab passing as we came out, and Holmes hailed it.

"How far to Wallington?" he asked.

"Only about a mile, sir."

"Very good. Jump in, Watson. We must strike while the iron is hot. Simple as the case is, there have been one or two very instructive details in connection with it. Just pull up at a telegraph office as you pass, cabby."

Holmes sent off a short wire and for the rest of the drive lay back in the cab, with his hat tilted over his nose to keep the sun from his face. Our drive pulled up at a house which was not unlike the one which we had just quitted. My companion ordered him to wait, and had his hand upon the knocker, when the door opened and a grave young gentleman in black, with a very shiny hat, appeared on the step.

"Is Miss Cushing at home?" asked Holmes.

"Miss Sarah Cushing is extremely ill," said he. "She has been suffering since yesterday from brain symptoms of great severity. As her medical adviser, I cannot possibly take the responsibility of allowing anyone to see her. I should recommend you to call again in ten days." He drew on his gloves, closed the door, and marched off down the street.

"Well, if we can't we can't," said Holmes, cheerfully.

"Perhaps she could not or would not have told you much."

"I did not wish her to tell me anything. I only wanted to look at her. However, I think that I have got all that I want. Drive us to some decent hotel, cabby, where we may have some lunch, and afterwards we shall drop down upon friend Lestrade at the police-station."

We had a pleasant little meal together, during which Holmes would talk about nothing but violins, narrating with great exultation how he had purchased his own Stradivarius, which was worth at least five hundred guineas, at a Jew broker's in Tottenham Court Road for fifty-five shillings. This led him to Paganini, and we sat for an hour over a bottle of claret while he told me anecdote after anecdote of that extraordinary man. The afternoon was far advanced and the hot glare had softened into a mellow glow before we found ourselves at the police-station. Lestrade was waiting for us at the door.

"A telegram for you, Mr Holmes," said he.

"Ha! It is the answer!" He tore it open, glanced his eyes over it, and crumpled it into his pocket. "That's all right," said he.

"Have you found out anything?"

"I have found out everything!"

"What!" Lestrade stared at him in amazement. "You are joking."

"I was never more serious in my life. A shocking crime has been committed, and I think I have now laid bare every detail of it."

"And the criminal?"

Holmes scribbled a few words upon the back of one of his visiting cards and threw it over to Lestrade.

"That is the name," he said. "You cannot effect an arrest until to-morrow night at the earliest. I should prefer that you do not mention my name at all in connection with the case, as I choose to be only associated with those crimes which present some difficulty in their solution. Come on, Watson." We strode off together to the station, leaving Lestrade still staring with a delighted face at the card which Holmes had thrown him.

"The case," said Sherlock Holmes as we chatted over our cigars that night in our rooms at Baker Street, "is one where, as in the investigations which you have chronicled under the names of 'A Study in Scarlet' and of 'The Sign of Four,' we have been compelled to reason backward from effects to causes. I have written to Lestrade asking him to supply us with the details which are now wanting, and which he will only get after he has secured his man. That he may be safely trusted to do, for although he is absolutely devoid of reason, he is as tenacious as a bulldog when he once understands what he has to do, and indeed, it is just this tenacity which has brought him to the top at Scotland Yard."

"Your case is not complete, then?" I asked.

"It is fairly complete in essentials. We know who the author of the revolting business is, although one of the victims still escapes us. Of course, you have formed your own conclusions."

"I presume that this Jim Browner, the steward of a Liverpool boat, is the man whom you suspect?"

"Oh! it is more than a suspicion."

"And yet I cannot see anything save very vague indications."

"On the contrary, to my mind nothing could be more clear. Let me run over the principal steps. We approached the case, you remember, with an absolutely blank mind, which is always an advantage. We had formed no theories. We were simply there to observe and to draw inferences from our observations. What did we see first? A very placid and respectable lady, who seemed quite innocent of any secret, and a portrait which showed me that she had two younger sisters. It instantly flashed across my mind that the box might have been meant for one of these. I set the idea aside as one which could be disproved or confirmed at our leisure. Then we went to the garden, as you remember, and we saw the very singular contents of the little yellow box.

"The string was of the quality which is used by sail-makers aboard ship, and at once a whiff of the sea was perceptible in our investigation. When I observed that the knot was one which is popular with sailors, that the parcel had been posted at a port, and that the male ear was pierced for an earring which is so much more common among sailors than landsmen, I was quite certain that all the actors in the tragedy were to be found among our seafaring classes.

"When I came to examine the address of the packet I observed that it was to Miss S. Cushing. Now, the oldest sister would, of course, be Miss Cushing, and although her initial was 'S' it might belong to one of the others as well. In that case we should have to commence our investigation from a fresh basis altogether. I therefore went into the house with the intention of clearing up this point. I was about to assure Miss Cushing that I was convinced that a mistake had been made when you may remember that I came suddenly to a stop. The fact was that I had just seen something which filled me with surprise and at the same time narrowed the field of our inquiry immensely.

"As a medical man, you are aware, Watson, that there is no part of the body which varies so much as the human ear. Each ear is as a rule quite distinctive and differs from all other ones. In last year's *Anthropological Journal* you will find two short monographs from my pen upon the subject. I had, therefore, examined the ears in the box with the eyes of an expert and had carefully noted their anatomical peculiarities. Imagine my surprise, then, when on looking at Miss Cushing I perceived that her ear corresponded exactly with the female ear which I had just inspected. The matter was entirely beyond coincidence. There was the same shortening of the pinna, the same broad curve of the upper lobe, the same convolution of the inner cartilage. In all essentials it was the same ear.

"In the first place, her sister's name was Sarah, and her address had until recently been the same, so that it was quite obvious how the mistake had occurred and for whom the packet was meant. Then we heard of this steward, married to the third sister, and learned that he had at one time been so intimate with Miss Sarah that she had actually gone up to Liverpool to be near the Browners, but a quarrel had afterwards divided them. This quarrel had put a stop to all communications for some months, so that if Browner had occasion to address a packet to Miss Sarah, he would undoubtedly have done so to her old address.

"And now the matter had begun to straighten itself out wonderfully. We had learned of the existence of this steward, an impulsive man, of strong passions—you remember that he threw up what must have been a very superior berth in order to be nearer to his wife—subject, too, to occasional fits of hard drinking. We had reason to believe that his wife had been murdered, and that a man—presumably a seafaring man—had been murdered at the same time. Jealousy, of course, at once suggests itself as the motive for the crime. And why should these proofs of the deed be sent to Miss Sarah Cushing? Probably because during her residence in Liverpool she had some hand in bringing about the events which led to the tragedy. You will observe that this line of boats call at Belfast, Dublin, and Waterford; so that, presuming that Browner had committed the deed and had embarked at once upon his steamer, the *May Day*, Belfast would be the first place at which he could post his terrible packet.

"A second solution was at this stage obviously possible, and although I thought it exceedingly unlikely, I was determined to elucidate it before going further. An unsuccessful lover might have killed Mr and Mrs Browner, and the male ear might have belonged to the husband. There were many grave objections to this theory, but it was conceivable. I therefore sent off a telegram to my friend Algar, of the Liverpool force, and asked him to find out if Mrs Browner were at home, and if Browner had departed in the *May Day*. Then we went on to Wallington to visit Miss Sarah.

"I was curious, in the first place, to see how far the family ear had been reproduced in her. Then, of course, she might give us very important information, but I was not sanguine that she would. She must have heard of the business the day before, since all Croydon was ringing with it, and she alone could have understood for whom the packet was meant. If she had been willing to help justice she would probably have communicated with the police already. However, it was clearly our duty to see her, so we went. We found that the news of the arrival of the packet—for her illness dated from that time—had such an effect upon her as to bring on brain fever. It was clearer than ever that she understood its full significance, but equally clear that we should have to wait some time for any assistance from her.

"However, we were really independent of her help. Our answers were waiting for us at the police-station, where I had directed Algar to send them. Nothing could be more conclusive. Mrs

Browner's house had been closed for more than three days, and the neighbours were of opinion that she had gone south to see her relatives. It had been ascertained at the shipping offices that Browner had left aboard the *May Day*, and I calculate that she is due in the Thames tomorrow night. When he arrives he will be met by the obtuse but resolute Lestrade, and I have no doubt that we shall have all our details filled in."

Sherlock Holmes was not disappointed in his expectations. Two days later he received a bulky envelope, which contained a short note from the detective, and a typewritten document, which covered several pages of foolscap.

"Lestrade has got him all right," said Holmes, glancing up at me. "Perhaps it would interest you to hear what he says.

My dear Mr Holmes:

In accordance with the scheme which we had formed in order to test our theories ["The 'we' is rather fine, Watson, is it not?"] I went down to the Albert Dock yesterday at 6 p.m., and boarded the S.S. *May Day*, belonging to the Liverpool, Dublin, and London Steam Packet Company. On inquiry, I found that there was a steward on board of the name of James Browner and that he had acted during the voyage in such an extraordinary manner that the captain had been compelled to relieve him of his duties. On descending to his berth, I found him seated upon a chest with his head sunk upon his hands, rocking himself to and fro. He is a big, powerful chap, clean-shaven, and very swarthy—something like Aldridge, who helped us in the bogus laundry affair. He jumped up when he heard my business, and I had my whistle to my lips to call a couple of river police, who were round the corner, but he seemed to have no heart in him, and he held out his hands quietly enough for the darbies. We brought him along to the cells, and his box as well, for we thought there might be something incriminating; but, bar a big sharp knife such as most sailors have, we got nothing for our trouble. However, we find that we shall want no more evidence, for on being brought before the inspector at the station he asked leave to make a statement, which was, of course, taken down, just as he made it, by our shorthand man. We had three copies typewritten, one of which I enclose. The affair proves, as I always thought it would, to be an extremely simple one, but I am obliged to you for assisting me in my investigation. With kind regards,

    Yours very truly,

    G. Lestrade.

"Hum! The investigation really was a very simple one," remarked Holmes, "but I don't think it struck him in that light when he first called us in. However, let us see what Jim Browner has to say for himself. This is his statement as made before Inspector Montgomery at the Shadwell Police Station, and it has the advantage of being verbatim."

"'Have I anything to say? Yes, I have a deal to say. I have to make a clean breast of it all. You can hang me, or you can leave me alone. I don't care a plug which you do. I tell you I've not shut an eye in sleep since I did it, and I don't believe I ever will again until I get past all waking. Sometimes it's his face, but most generally it's hers. I'm never without one or the other before me. He looks frowning and black-like, but she has a kind o' surprise upon her face. Ay, the white lamb, she might well be surprised when she read death on a face that had seldom looked anything but love upon her before.

"'But it was Sarah's fault, and may the curse of a broken man put a blight on her and set the blood rotting in her veins! It's not that I want to clear myself. I know that I went back to drink, like the beast that I was. But she would have forgiven me; she would have stuck as close to me a rope to a block if that woman had never darkened our door. For Sarah Cushing loved me—that's the root of the business—she loved me until all her love turned to poisonous hate when she knew that I thought more of my wife's footmark in the mud than I did of her whole body and soul.

"'There were three sisters altogether. The old one was just a good woman, the second was a devil, and the third was an angel. Sarah was thirty-three, and Mary was twenty-nine when I married. We were just as happy as the day was long when we set up house together, and in all Liverpool there was no better woman than my Mary. And then we asked Sarah up for a week, and the week grew into a month, and one thing led to another, until she was just one of ourselves.

"'I was blue ribbon at that time, and we were putting a little money by, and all was as bright as a new dollar. My God, whoever would have thought that it could have come to this? Whoever would have dreamed it?

"'I used to be home for the week-ends very often, and sometimes if the ship were held back for cargo I would have a whole week at a time, and in this way I saw a deal of my sister-in-law, Sarah. She was a fine tall woman, black and quick and fierce, with a proud way of carrying her head, and a glint from her eye like a spark from a flint. But when little Mary was there I had never a thought of her, and that I swear as I hope for God's mercy.

"'It had seemed to me sometimes that she liked to be alone with me, or to coax me out for a walk with her, but I had never thought anything of that. But one evening my eyes were opened. I had come up from the ship and found my wife out, but Sarah at home. "Where's Mary?" I asked. "Oh, she has gone to pay some accounts." I was impatient and paced up and down the room. "Can't you be happy for five minutes without Mary, Jim?" says she. "It's a bad compliment to me that you can't be contented with my society for so short a time." "That's all right, my lass," said I, putting out my hand towards her in a kindly way, but she had it in both hers in an instant, and they burned as if they were in a fever. I looked into her eyes and I read it all there. There was no need for her to speak, nor for me either. I frowned and drew my hand away. Then she stood by my side in silence for a bit, and then put up her hand and patted me on the shoulder. "Steady old Jim!" said she, and with a kind o' mocking laugh, she ran out of the room.

"'Well, from that time Sarah hated me with her whole heart and soul, and she is a woman who can hate, too. I was a fool to let her go on biding with us—a besotted fool—but I never said a word to Mary, for I knew it would grieve her. Things went on much as before, but after a time I began to find that there was a bit of a change in Mary herself. She had always been so trusting and so innocent, but now she became queer and suspicious, wanting to know where I had been and what I had been doing, and whom my letters were from, and what I had in my pockets, and a thousand such follies. Day by day she grew queerer and more irritable, and we had ceaseless rows about nothing. I was fairly puzzled by it all. Sarah avoided me now, but she and Mary were just inseparable. I can see now how she was plotting and scheming and poisoning my wife's mind against me, but I was such a blind beetle that I could not understand it at the time. Then I broke my blue ribbon and began to drink again, but I think I should not have done it if Mary had been the same as ever. She had some reason to be disgusted with me now, and the gap between us began to be wider and wider. And then this Alec Fairbairn chipped in, and things became a thousand times blacker.

"'It was to see Sarah that he came to my house first, but soon it was to see us, for he was a man with winning ways, and he made friends wherever he went. He was a dashing, swaggering chap, smart and curled, who had seen half the world and could talk of what he had seen. He was good company, I won't deny it, and he had wonderful polite ways with him for a sailor man, so that I think there must have been a time when he knew more of the poop than the forecastle. For a month he was in and out of my house, and never once did it cross my mind that harm might come of his soft, tricky ways. And then at last something made me suspect, and from that day my peace was gone forever.

"'It was only a little thing, too. I had come into the parlour unexpected, and as I walked in at the door I saw a light of welcome on my wife's face. But as she saw who it was it faded again, and she turned away with a look of disappointment. That was enough for me. There was no one but Alec Fairbairn whose step she could have mistaken for mine. If I could have seen him then I should have killed him, for I have always been like a madman when my temper gets loose. Mary saw the devil's light in my eyes, and she ran forward with her hands on my sleeve. "Don't, Jim, don't!" says she. "Where's Sarah?" I asked. "In the kitchen," says she. "Sarah," says I as I went in, "this man Fairbairn is never to darken my door again." "Why not?" says she. "Because I order it." "Oh!" says she, "if my friends are not good enough for this house, then I am not good enough for it either." "You can do what you like," says I, "but if Fairbairn shows his face here again I'll send you one of his ears for a keepsake." She was frightened by my face, I think, for she never answered a word, and the same evening she left my house.

"'Well, I don't know now whether it was pure devilry on the part of this woman, or whether she thought that she could turn me against my wife by encouraging her to misbehave. Anyway, she took a house just two streets off and let lodgings to sailors. Fairbairn used to stay there, and Mary would go round to have tea with her sister and him. How often she went I don't know, but I followed her one day, and as I broke in at the door Fairbairn got away over the back garden wall, like the cowardly skunk that he was. I swore to my wife that I would kill her if I found her in his company again, and I led her back with me, sobbing and trembling, and as white as a piece of paper. There was no trace of love between us any longer. I could see that she hated me and feared me, and when the thought of it drove me to drink, then she despised me as well.

"'Well, Sarah found that she could not make a living in Liverpool, so she went back, as I understand, to live with her sister in Croydon, and things jogged on much the same as ever at home. And then came this week and all the misery and ruin.

"'It was in this way. We had gone on the *May Day* for a round voyage of seven days, but a hogshead got loose and started one of our plates, so that we had to put back into port for twelve hours. I left the ship and came home, thinking what a surprise it would be for my wife, and hoping that maybe she would be glad to see me so soon. The thought was in my head as I turned into my own street, and at that moment a cab passed me, and there she was, sitting by the side of Fairbairn, the two chatting and laughing, with never a thought for me as I stood watching them from the footpath.

"'I tell you, and I give you my word for it, that from that moment I was not my own master, and it is all like a dim dream when I look back on it. I had been drinking hard of late, and the two things together fairly turned my brain. There's something throbbing in my head now, like a docker's hammer, but that morning I seemed to have all Niagara whizzing and buzzing in my ears.

"'Well, I took to my heels, and I ran after the cab. I had a heavy oak stick in my hand, and I tell you I saw red from the first; but as I ran I got cunning, too, and hung back a little to see them without being seen. They pulled up soon at the railway station. There was a good crowd round the booking-office, so I got quite close to them without being seen. They took tickets for New Brighton. So did I, but I got in three carriages behind them. When we reached it they walked along the Parade, and I was never more than a hundred yards from them. At last I saw them hire a boat and start for a row, for it was a very hot day, and they thought, no doubt, that it would be cooler on the water.

"'It was just as if they had been given into my hands. There was a bit of a haze, and you could not see more than a few hundred yards. I hired a boat for myself, and I pulled after them. I could see the blur of their craft, but they were going nearly as fast as I, and they must have been a long mile from the shore before I caught them up. The haze was like a curtain all round us, and there were we three in the middle of it. My God, shall I ever forget their faces when they saw who was in the boat that was closing in upon them? She screamed out. He swore like a madman and jabbed at me with an oar, for he must have seen death in my eyes. I got past it and got one in with my stick that crushed his head like an egg. I would have spared her, perhaps, for all my madness, but she threw her arms round him, crying out to him, and calling him "Alec." I struck again, and she lay stretched beside him. I was like a wild beast then that had tasted blood. If Sarah had been there, by the Lord, she should have joined them. I pulled out my knife, and—well, there! I've said enough. It gave me a kind of savage joy when I thought how Sarah would feel when she had such signs as these of what her meddling had brought about. Then I tied the bodies into the boat, stove a plank, and stood by until they had sunk. I knew very well that the owner would think that they had lost their bearings in the haze, and had drifted off out to sea. I cleaned myself up, got back to land, and joined my ship without a soul having a suspicion of what had passed. That night I made up the packet for Sarah Cushing, and next day I sent it from Belfast.

"'There you have the whole truth of it. You can hang me, or do what you like with me, but you cannot punish me as I have been punished already. I cannot shut my eyes but I see those two faces staring at me—staring at me as they stared when my boat broke through the haze. I killed them quick, but they are killing me slow; and if I have another night of it I shall be either mad or dead before morning. You won't put me alone into a cell, sir? For pity's sake don't, and may you be treated in your day of agony as you treat me now.'

"What is the meaning of it, Watson?" said Holmes solemnly as he laid down the paper. "What object is served by this circle of misery and violence and fear? It must tend to some end, or else our universe is ruled by chance, which is unthinkable. But what end? There is the great standing perennial problem to which human reason is as far from an answer as ever."

✗

COMING NEXT TIME . . .

STORIES! ARTICLES!
SHERLOCK HOLMES & DR. WATSON!

Sherlock Holmes Mystery Magazine #23 is just a few months away...watch for it!

Not a subscriber yet?
Send $59.95 for 6 issues (postage paid in the U.S.) to:

Wildside Press LLC
Attn: Subscription Dept.
9710 Traville Gateway Dr. #234
Rockville MD 20850

You can also subscribe online at wildsidepress.com

www.ingramcontent.com/pod-product-compliance
Lightning Source LLC
Chambersburg PA
CBHW031834170626
46807CB00004B/1453